Shoofly
Die

Jan Fields

Annie's®
AnniesFiction.com

Books in the Chocolate Shoppe Mysteries series

Library of Congress-in-Publication Data
Shoofly Die / by Jan Fields
p. cm.
I. Title
2018950339

AnniesFiction.com
(800) 282-6643
Chocolate Shoppe Mysteries™
Series Creator: Shari Lohner
Series Editor: Elizabeth Morrissey
Cover Illustrator: Bonnie Leick

10 11 12 13 14 | Printed in South Korea | 9 8 7 6 5 4 3

As Jillian Green stood in the storage room of The Chocolate Shoppe Bakery, she marveled, as she often did, at how clean everything was. This was a room where they kept sacks of flour and sugar, substances that tended to float around until they covered every surface—but not in this bakery. Jillian's grandmother, Bertie Harper, believed that health codes were rather lax, and she made sure everyone who worked there abided by the same standard. As a result, the storage room, with its floor-to-ceiling shelves, had less dust than the top of Jillian's dresser at home.

Cleanliness wasn't the only rule in the storage room. The organization of every bag, box, and can was equally exacting. Jillian thought it resembled a stage set, an imitation of real life without the mess. All the supplies the bakery used regularly were on the lowest shelves, as the system had been designed by a very short baker. The top shelves held overflow, so when the lower shelves were depleted, someone could restock them from the goods higher up. Usually that someone was veteran Chocolate Shoppe employee Lenora Ryan, who was taller than Jillian, but Lenora was washing baking trays at the moment. They'd just used up the last of the flour from the lower shelves, so Jillian had volunteered to bring down a few heavy bags of flour from the top shelf to refill the rolling metal bin in the kitchen.

Unfortunately, no matter how neat or organized her grand-mother was, she couldn't quite combat the chaos of other people. The step stool that belonged folded and slid into the space between two of the sets of shelves was missing. Jillian suspected she knew where it was. Only the day before, she'd seen their countergirl,

Maggie, standing on the stool and swapping out some of the seasonal decor that perched atop the tall display of day-old bargains. *Nothing says fall like a basket of foam gourds on top of a rack of half-price pumpkin bread,* Jillian thought.

That meant the stool was probably behind the front counter. Jillian could go get the stool and drag it back to the storage room, thereby making this chore the tiniest bit longer and giving Bertie something to grumble about. Or she could do what she'd done years before when she'd helped out at the bakery as a teen and scale the shelves themselves to reach the surplus bags of flour at the top.

Jillian wasn't a teenager anymore, but she was sure she could still manage the climb. The shelves were securely fastened at floor and ceiling. They were sturdily built, so she knew they could take her weight without any problem. She grabbed the rough wood of the shelf supports, careful not to run her hand along the planks. She'd picked more than her share of splinters out of her hand by doing that.

She bounced on her toes, then lifted a leg for the first shelf. It was higher than she'd remembered, but she managed it, albeit with a bit more groaning than the last time she'd made this climb. Now she could reach the bags piled on the top shelf.

Grinning, Jillian stretched with one hand to pull the closest bag of flour toward her. She knew from experience to brace for the weight. Flour sacks were heavy.

What she hadn't planned on was that flour sacks were not quite as sturdy as when she was a teenager. The rough planking of the shelves resisted her tug on the bag, so she pulled harder. When Jillian gave a last hard yank, the bag ripped wide open, dousing her in a cloud of white flour.

Jillian was shocked at the sudden flour bath and she tumbled off the shelf, pulling the ripped bag along with her. It poured out still more flour as Jillian landed in a heap on the floor.

Flour filled the air like a toxic gas, making Jillian cough and gasp. She scrambled to her feet and staggered out of the storage room, desperate for the clean oxygen in the narrow hallway behind the kitchen where rolling appliances and racks were kept when not in use.

Jillian doubled over and placed her hands on her thighs as she tried to cough the flour out of her lungs. She knew she'd have to wait until the flour settled in the storeroom before she could clean it up or else she'd end up asphyxiating.

She was just beginning to feel normal when the bakery's back door clicked open. Jillian straightened, wondering who was coming through the rear entry. At the same instant, Lenora walked into the hallway from the kitchen, a stack of sheet trays in her arms, no doubt intending to load them into one of the racks near Jillian.

Before Lenora could turn her way, Jillian opened her mouth to say something to her. Then, the back door swung open and Jillian's great-aunt, Cornelia Montgomery, walked in, pulling Jillian's attention away from Lenora.

Cornelia spotted Jillian and shrieked, "A haint!"

The scream pulled Lenora's focus away from the trays she was carrying, and she caught sight of Jillian. She shrieked, throwing the trays into the air. The resulting clatter was nearly deafening.

As soon as she stood a chance of being heard over the hollering and clanging, Jillian yelled, "It's me! Stop screaming."

"Jillian Green!" Lenora shouted. "What are you doing? Don't you know I'm an old woman? You could have given me a heart attack."

Though Lenora was at least twenty years older than Jillian, she could hardly be considered an old woman. She was tall and strong from years of lifting heavy pans at the bakery. She'd worked for The Chocolate Shoppe for as long as Jillian could remember. She was family—very grumpy family at the moment.

Cornelia put her hands on her thin hips. "Your silly prank

didn't scare me any. I could tell it was you right away."

"Which is no doubt why you yelled, 'haint,'" Jillian said drily, then she coughed again. Before she could explain any further about why she was in the condition she was, Bertie walked into the hallway and crossed her arms over her chest.

Now Jillian was facing nearly identical scowls from her grandmother and Cornelia, who were twins with drastically different personalities. "What are you doing, playing games back here?" Bertie asked Jillian. "Do you not have enough work to do?"

"I wasn't playing games," Jillian insisted. She gestured to her flour-covered clothes. "This isn't my idea of fun." She began beating the flour out of her shirt and apron as she explained about the incident in the storage room.

"Stop that." Bertie flapped a hand at her. "You'll get flour all over back here. You should change and clean up the storage room."

"Maybe not in that order," Lenora suggested helpfully as she picked up the trays from the floor. She tapped one with a finger. "Now I'm going to have to wash these again."

At Lenora's accusatory tone, Jillian felt the need to defend herself again. "It was an accident," she said, but the words hit Lenora's back as the tall woman carried the trays back to the front of the kitchen for washing.

"An accident you could have avoided by not climbing shelves," Bertie pointed out. Then she faced her sister. "What are you doing here?"

Cornelia raised her chin. "Can't I come to town to visit my sister and niece at work?"

"Without an ulterior motive?" Bertie asked. "Not likely."

Cornelia shrugged. "Actually, I wanted to tell you about this." She held up a piece of paper and waved it. "I saw this flyer at the Clip & Curl. You know the old Horse Ridge Mill building?"

"The one someone's been working on?" Bertie asked.

"It's a theater now," Cornelia said excitedly. "And not a movie theater, either. A real theater. And there is going to be a musical right there. The director has actually been on Broadway. Apparently, the musical is a murder mystery, and it will be premiering right here in Moss Hollow."

"That's pretty far off Broadway," Jillian said.

"Yes, the women at the salon thought maybe the director was searching for a fresh new location. New York City is terribly predictable."

"Have you ever been to New York City?" Jillian asked.

Cornelia sniffed. "Of course. Well, sort of. Raymond and I went to Niagara Falls once, and that's in New York."

Jillian didn't even know what to say in response to that, so she went back to dusting off her clothes.

"I assume from your excitement that you intend to audition for something?" Bertie asked.

"Yes," Cornelia said, her eyes sparkling. "There is a part of a wealthy older woman. I think I would be perfect for that. My Raymond always said I exuded class."

Jillian had to admit that her aunt was a classy woman. A little nutty and eccentric, but elegant and graceful all the same. "I think that would be a good match. Will you have to sing?" She had heard Cornelia sing. She wasn't sure it was her greatest gift.

"I imagine so," Cornelia said. "It is a musical, after all. I'll practice my scales." She launched into one right there, and Jillian winced. Then Cornelia stopped and pointed the flyer at Jillian. "You should audition too. I think you would be wonderful in the female lead. I mean, this is a murder mystery. It's perfect for you. You already have plenty of real-world experience."

Jillian resisted the urge to roll her eyes. Under no circumstances was amateur sleuthing a prerequisite to acting in a stage musical. "I'm completely sure that no role in a musical is perfect for me."

"Oh, don't be silly. Come out and have a coffee with me. I'll tell you all about it." She linked an arm through Jillian's flour-coated one and began towing her along.

Jillian resisted. "Aunt Cornelia, I need to clean up the storage room."

Bertie walked over and poked her head into the storeroom, then raised an eyebrow at Jillian. "Go have a coffee with your aunt," she said. "It's going to be awhile before all that flour is done settling."

With a sigh, Jillian let Cornelia guide her the rest of the way through the kitchen and out into the bakery's customer area. Jillian expected Cornelia to pause at the coffee maker, but instead, she let go of Jillian's arm and rushed past the front counter.

"Are you with the theater?" Cornelia asked, hurrying up to a willowy blonde and gesturing at a bundle of papers in the woman's hand. Jillian saw they were copies of the same flyer Cornelia held.

The young woman smiled tightly. "I am Brittany Blaine. It is my theater, and I'm writing and directing our first show."

Cornelia clapped her hands, though the sound was muffled by the paper she still held. "I'm so pleased. I'm going to audition for your play. I understand you need a wealthy matron." She waved a hand toward Jillian. "And I thought my niece might audition for the lead."

Brittany Blaine examined Jillian slowly, starting at the toes of her sneakers and ending at the top of her head. It was all Jillian could do not to brush at the flour on her clothes as she sensed the bemusement in the woman's glance. The perfectly coiffed blonde was impeccably dressed in an outfit that Jillian recognized as pricey. She knew how rumpled and dirty she looked in comparison.

"I'm not sure the lead is right for you," Brittany said with a smile that bordered on condescending. "I was planning to cast someone younger. Perhaps you could try for the role of the housekeeper. She's older and quite matronly." She held out a flyer to Jillian.

Jillian didn't even glance down at the woman's hand, though she'd already noticed Brittany's absolutely perfect manicure. "I wasn't planning to audition for *any* parts. Thank you." And with that, she spun on her heel and stomped back to the kitchen, embarrassingly aware that her clothes were releasing tiny puffs of flour with every step.

Behind her, she heard Brittany let out a girlish giggle. "Well, she certainly has the actor's temperament down anyway."

On the way back to the storeroom, Jillian grumbled under her breath. She couldn't believe the woman's attitude. It reminded Jillian of a few of the people she'd come into contact with in her past life working in advertising in California, people who acted as if Jillian's Southern accent came with some kind of brain damage. Back then, she'd showed them the error of underestimating her, but now she doubted there was anything she had or could do that would impress Brittany Blaine.

"Who tied a knot in your tail?" Lenora asked.

Lenora's wide brown eyes were alight with amusement, and Jillian wasn't sure she'd find much sympathy there. Still, she wanted to complain to someone. "Aunt Cornelia's idol is out in the customer area."

Lenora laughed. "And who would that be?"

"The owner of the new theater." Jillian crossed her arms, trying to ignore the flour that radiated from her when she did. "And the woman said I should try out for one of the old lady roles."

"I hate to get in the way of a good sulk," Lenora said, her voice still full of suppressed laughter, "but you should probably go up to my apartment and grab a shower. Right now, your hair is all white and you have flour caked in every line on your face. I love you like my own child, but you are a fright."

Jillian put her hand to her cheek, feeling the dry, dusty flour still coating her skin. "Thanks. I think I will. And I promise not to leave your shower dirty."

Lenora flapped a hand at her. "Go on. Just don't lean on the shower wall once you get all that flour wet. You'll paste yourself right to the tiles." She chuckled heartily, and Jillian left her to her entertainment. She walked through the storage room and then up the stairs to Lenora's apartment.

As always, she enjoyed the quiet hominess of the tiny residence. A neat braided rug in the middle of the floor and a crocheted afghan draped over the love seat gave the otherwise uncluttered room a cozy feel. Jillian walked slowly and carefully so she wouldn't leave a flour trail in her wake.

Once she reached the bathroom, she peered into the wood-framed mirror over the sink. The woman who stared back at her was nearly unrecognizable. Lines Jillian barely knew she had were now deep, white wrinkles, and her wild, red curls were matted down and coated in powder. Jillian admitted to herself that she definitely looked older. Maybe Brittany had honestly misjudged her age and wasn't simply being catty.

"I still don't want to be in the play," she told her reflection. Still, she would probably go to the auditions to lend Cornelia moral support. *And who knows? A musical theater production might be good for Moss Hollow and lots of fun to watch.*

Jillian smiled, and a hunk of caked-on flour fell off into the sink. She hoped that wasn't an omen.

2

On Saturday, Cornelia was positively vibrating with anxiety and excitement. "Do you think this dress conveys elegance and sophistication?" she asked Jillian as they walked out the wide front door of Belle Haven, the antebellum mansion they called home.

Jillian thought the dress mostly conveyed her great-aunt's love of floral patterns, but she was hardly going to say that considering Cornelia had already changed clothes three times. "I think it's lovely."

"But when you look at me, do you think 'wealthy dowager'?" Cornelia asked. "One who might be capable of murder?"

"I don't know," Jillian said. "I don't think I know any wealthy dowagers to judge by."

Cornelia frowned down at the silky fabric of her sleeve. "I should wear the black dress. It's not the best with my coloring, but it makes me look more dangerous." She started to turn, but Jillian caught her arm.

"You should wear this dress," Jillian said. "The black one doesn't show off your natural beauty as well." She worried that she was laying it on a little thick, but she really didn't want to stand around while Cornelia swapped her outfit again.

Cornelia smoothed the skirt of her dress. "You're right. Let's go."

With relief, Jillian hustled Cornelia toward her snow-white Prius, but Cornelia ground to a stop. "Not your car, darling," she said. "Your seats are too small and my dress will get creased. We'll take my car, but you can drive. I'll run through my vocal exercises." She launched into a series of odd sounds that reminded Jillian of the bird exhibits at the zoo in Atlanta.

Jillian winced at the sound but didn't comment. She walked

with Cornelia to the meticulously restored powder-blue Mustang that had been one of Uncle Raymond's prized possessions. The car was challenging to drive, but Cornelia wouldn't hear of selling anything Raymond had loved so much.

The ride to the theater involved more vocal exercises, and Jillian's ears were ringing by the time they pulled into the freshly paved lot in front of the old Horse Ridge Mill building. Jillian hadn't driven by the abandoned mill during the remodeling, but she remembered it from before, when bricks were missing and the rain gutters had hung like rusty garland. Now that its renovation was complete, Jillian was glad to see that, although the structure seemed significantly brighter, it had lost none of the charm of the old architecture.

Even before Jillian shut off the car, Cornelia had her door swung open. She scrambled out of the Mustang, clutching a folder that held her résumé and head shot. The photo had actually been taken with Jillian's phone after Bertie had talked Cornelia out of an expensive photo shoot. The bakery was doing well, but they still had to be conscientious about their spending, something Cornelia wasn't always good at.

Jillian had to trot to catch up with Cornelia before they reached the theater's front door, above which hung a vinyl banner emblazoned with *Opening Soon: Horse Ridge Theater* in bold lettering. Any resemblance to an old mill disappeared as soon as they passed into the beautifully decorated lobby. The floor was honey-hued hardwood, and, based on the patina and character, Jillian suspected that it was reclaimed pine. A curved staircase with a metal-and-wood banister led to the balcony level, the sweep of it matching the curve of the ticket counter. Much of the rest of the room was empty, aside from the dozens of prospective actors milling about, but Jillian suspected that wouldn't be the case by the time the play opened.

While Jillian was still looking around, she heard someone call her great-aunt's name. A small group of women from Cornelia's gardening club stood near the balcony stairs, and they waved their friend over. Cornelia hurried to join them without a glance back at Jillian.

Jillian chuckled. *So much for Cornelia needing moral support.* She jumped as someone tapped her shoulder. Spinning around, she found her best friend, Savannah Cantrell Wilson, grinning at her.

After an enthusiastic hug, Jillian asked, "Are you auditioning for the play?"

"I am." Savannah rocked on her toes, her nervous energy reminding Jillian of Cornelia. "It's all very exciting, don't you think? What part are you hoping for?"

"Audience member," Jillian said. "I'm not really the performing type. And I'm surprised to see you here. I wouldn't think you'd have time. Doesn't this sort of thing require tons of rehearsing?" Jillian gave her friend a teasing grin. "Won't your new husband miss you?"

"Actually, it was James's idea. He hears me sing around the bungalow and says everyone should get to hear it." Savannah blushed a little.

"Then shouldn't James be here offering moral support?" Jillian asked.

"He would be, but he had to work." Savannah's cheeks pinked still more. "He already bought me flowers to congratulate me on auditioning."

Jillian realized she felt a tiny pang of jealousy. Not that she wanted James, whom she'd actually dated many, many years before. She couldn't be happier with her current beau, the handsome Hunter Greyson. Still, Savannah had that newlywed glow, and while Jillian didn't begrudge her friend such blissful happiness, she had to confess she was a little envious.

Jillian suppressed a wistful sigh and linked arms with Savannah. "How many of the folks here do you suppose are actually auditioning, as opposed to checking out the new theater? I would never have guessed that there were this many citizens of Moss Hollow who believed they could sing or dance." She shuddered at the thought of doing either in front of all these people.

Savannah glanced at the crowd. "I imagine at least half are here to watch or offer moral support."

"I hope so, otherwise we'll probably be here all day."

"Maybe," Savannah said, her eyes sparkling. "But what an exciting way to spend a Saturday." And with that, the two walked on into the theater.

With a style similar to the lobby, the theater itself was lovely. Jillian knew the transformation from mill to theater must have been expensive, especially since the end result gave the impression that the building had always been a theater. Wooden beams and warm lighting gave the cavernous space a cozy yet luxurious feel, as did the classic theater seats upholstered in red velvet and the plush carpet under her feet.

Jillian's gaze swept the space as she followed Savannah, and she spotted Cornelia sidling into a row just ahead with her gardening group. Savannah headed past the row where Cornelia sat chatting and chose a seat quite a bit closer to the front than Jillian would have selected. As Jillian settled into her chair, she was amazed at how comfortable the seats were. Truly little expense had been spared in this theater. *Ms. Blaine must have backers with very deep pockets.*

Up on the stage, the woman in question chatted with several people Jillian recognized, including the mayor of Moss Hollow. "Do you suppose Mayor Blackwater is going to be in the play?" she whispered to Savannah.

"Hard to say," Savannah answered. "Judging by his speaking

voice, he must sing baritone. But really, Mayor Blackwater doesn't miss too many public events. This play has been the talk of the town, and he could just be here making an appearance."

Jillian watched Brittany as she talked, her face animated and her hands moving constantly, making a heavy load of rings flash in the stage lights. She was certainly an attractive woman, Jillian mused, then corrected herself. Sure, Brittany was beautiful, but there was nothing attractive about the haughty expression she aimed at her small audience on the stage.

Jillian was so caught up in watching Brittany that she jumped when someone settled into the seat beside her. Jillian twisted in her chair, expecting to see Cornelia, imagining that her great-aunt must have felt guilty about abandoning Jillian. Instead, she found herself looking into a familiar pair of bright blue eyes.

"Hunter!" she exclaimed, squeezing his hand as he took hers. "I didn't expect you to be here."

"I didn't expect to be," he said. Then, to Jillian's surprise, he actually flushed. "I met Miss Blaine at Food for Less and she talked me into auditioning for the lead. She's got a rather forceful personality."

Jillian wasn't completely sure she was comfortable with the idea of Brittany turning her "forceful" personality on Hunter. Admittedly, it made sense for him to try out. He had leading-man good looks, and she knew he had a good voice. In fact, he'd joined the church choir because of his love of singing.

"Do you have time for this?" she asked. She knew running the local funeral home kept Hunter every bit as busy as the bakery did Jillian.

"I don't know, really. I hope so. I have help at Greyson & Sons, and Miss Blaine promised they would work around my schedule as much as possible."

Jillian was startled by that. Brittany didn't seem to be the type of person interested in accommodating the needs of anyone other than herself. Clearly, she really wanted Hunter in the play. Jillian felt a small chill of worry. *What if Brittany really wants Hunter, period?*

"Is something wrong?" Hunter asked with his usual perception.

Jillian smiled, hoping it appeared more convincing than it felt. It was silly to worry about Hunter and another woman. She trusted him completely. If Hunter ever decided he didn't want to be with Jillian, he'd be open and honest about it. And it wouldn't be because some other woman had come to town. "I'm just a little stunned, I think. I didn't realize so many people were comfortable with the idea of dancing and singing in front of an audience."

Hunter laughed. "I can't say I'm completely comfortable with it, but I do like to dance. And I've grown used to singing in front of people from my time in the choir." His expression grew wistful. "My father shared his love of music with me and always enjoyed my singing. It's part of what made me join the church choir—a kind of memorial to my dad. This would be more of that."

Jillian gave his hand a squeeze. "If you do take the role, I wish your dad could be here to see you perform. Or your mom. Maybe she'll fly in for the performance." Hunter's mother, Bernadette, was a pottery artist in New Mexico, and Jillian knew Hunter had a warm relationship with her. She kind of envied that, actually, since her relationship with her own parents, who lived out of an Airstream trailer while traveling the country, was nearly nonexistent these days.

"I don't think she can," he said. "She stays pretty busy this time of year. And we're jumping the gun pretty hard here. I shouldn't be acting as if I have the role automatically. There are some fine singers in Moss Hollow."

Jillian smiled at his modesty. *But none are as handsome as you.*

Movement on the stage drew Jillian's attention. Brittany's small entourage filed off the stage as she walked to a microphone on a stand at the center. Brittany held a clipboard in one hand and used it to gesture across the audience as she spread her arms.

Before she spoke, a gunshot rang out.

The audience screamed.

Brittany crumpled gracefully to the stage floor.

Screams echoed in the theater, and everyone moved at once. About half the audience immediately dove from their seats to crouch on the floor behind the relative protection of the seat backs in front of them. Some of the people who'd been seated near the aisles scrambled to make a run for the doors at the back of the theater. Jillian hoped no one got trampled in the desperate rush.

With Savannah and Hunter, Jillian headed toward the stage and the woman lying on it. Jillian didn't see any sign of blood and hoped that was good. In the crush of people in the aisle, they'd barely made it clear of their row when Brittany sat up. She smiled over the hysterical audience and raised her hand in a wave. Then she stood.

Jillian froze, stunned, as Brittany stepped to the microphone and asked everyone to be calm. "I was only setting the mood for the murder mystery that you'll be auditioning for," she said, her dazzling white teeth on full display as she grinned broadly. "I will want to see a performance that affects the audience as strongly as my little display affected you."

Jillian heard an angry murmur radiate through the large room. *I don't blame them for being upset. Someone could have been seriously injured in that irresponsible stunt.*

As if she couldn't hear the grumbling, Brittany waved at the wings of the stage. "I'd like to introduce you to the man who provided the thrill today: my stage manager, Porter Logan."

The long-legged man who strode across the stage barely glanced at the audience. His focus was entirely on Brittany as he took his place beside her. Jillian shuddered at the sight of the large handgun he held. Brittany took it from him and held it up. "This is a prop from our show, 'Murderous Intentions.' It's a real gun, but the sound you heard was only a blank, I assure you. Isn't that right, Porter?"

The tall, thin man bobbed his head without speaking. A lock of dark hair fell over his eyes.

Brittany laughed. "Porter's a little shy, but he's one of the best stage managers in the business. Now, if you all will take your seats, we'll get started with the auditions."

Hunter took Jillian's hand as they moved back to their row. Jillian was still horrified by the dangerous stunt, but she saw that nearly everyone followed Brittany's direction and returned to their seats. She only spotted a few people near the back of the theater who left.

Brittany tapped her clipboard. "I'm going to call out the first ten people. I only need one person at a time on stage, but I want you to be ready for your turn so we can keep the auditions moving. You may sing the selection you've prepared, and I'll let you know when I've heard enough." She took the microphone from the stand and walked over to a folding chair placed on the stage. After sitting down, she read off the first ten names.

Clearly the list wasn't in alphabetical order, as two of the first were Bree Weston, an employee with the Moss Hollow Parks Department, and Gordon Sprague, a retired high-school math teacher who used to hang out at the bakery. He'd mostly given up that habit when he realized Bertie was never going to date him.

To Jillian's surprise, Gordon sang wonderfully in a deep, clear baritone, and Bree's beautiful voice reminded her of a cartoon princess. Jillian rooted for everyone, even the people who apparently had considerably higher opinions of their singing skills than they probably should.

Brittany didn't give anyone much time as she made her way

down her list. Some folks she cut off so quickly that Jillian felt bad for them.

Finally, it was Hunter's turn to audition. Jillian sat at the edge of her seat, willing him to do well. He did. To Jillian's delight, he directed his romantic song toward her in the audience, barely glancing at anyone else, including Brittany. That didn't go unnoticed, and Brittany glared toward Jillian more than once.

Gripping her clipboard to her chest, Brittany hopped out of her seat. "That's fine, Hunter. I will need to hear you do one of the songs from the play in a moment." She scowled out across the audience. "I do want to say right now that if the audience continues to distract the performers, I will hold closed auditions for the rest of the day."

Since the room had been almost perfectly quiet during each performance, Jillian suspected the message was directed at her. She saw many of the other people around her exchange confused expressions.

Jillian simply folded her arms over her chest and glared back at Brittany. Seconds passed as their expressions locked in a battle of wills. Brittany gave up first, and she aimed a cloying smile at Hunter. "When you're ready, go ahead with one of the selections I gave you the music for when we chatted the other day. And kindly keep your attention on stage."

Hunter seemed puzzled, but he launched into the ballad as soon as Brittany sat down again. Jillian didn't much enjoy the idea of Hunter working with a woman who was clearly interested in more than his singing voice, but she couldn't argue that he was wonderful. She would have picked him for the lead, so she couldn't fault Brittany's taste.

Movement at the edge of the stage near the wings drew Jillian's attention away from Hunter. She spotted Porter Logan. He had his arms crossed as tightly as Jillian but it wasn't Brittany that drew

Porter's ire—it was Hunter. As he watched Hunter sing, Porter's expression was pure hatred. After a few moments, he stepped back out of Jillian's line of sight. Jillian leaned forward, trying to catch sight of him again, but he didn't reappear.

When Hunter finished his song, Brittany had him waltz around the stage with her. Though Jillian was disgusted with the way Brittany pressed against Hunter, she couldn't deny that they made a handsome couple. Hunter's thick, silver-streaked dark hair contrasted well with Brittany's golden chignon. As they circled the stage, Jillian realized she was clenching her teeth, and she yawned to loosen the muscles.

Savannah leaned close to her. "That woman certainly isn't subtle."

"No indeed."

Something in her tone must have surprised Savannah. "Jillian Green, you're not jealous of her, are you? Hunter adores you. Everyone in Moss Hollow knows how he feels."

"Miss Blaine seems to have missed the memo," Jillian said tightly.

Savannah laughed softly. "I think not. I saw the look she gave you."

Finally, Hunter pulled away from Brittany on the stage, murmuring something the audience couldn't hear. Brittany frowned a bit and nodded.

"Let's have one more selection, Hunter," she said. "If you don't mind. Anything you like."

Hunter flipped the page on his music and began singing. This song wasn't from the play, Jillian knew, and she nearly laughed.

"Shoo, fly, don't bother me," Hunter sang out in his clear tenor, focusing directly on Brittany as she'd insisted for the previous song. This time, she seemed less than happy at the serenade. "Shoo, fly, don't bother me. Shoo, fly, don't bother me." Hunter shot a mischievous smile toward Jillian. "For I belong to somebody."

The audience laughed aloud as he finished the jaunty song,

and several people clapped. Brittany gave Hunter a rather weak smile. She walked to the microphone. "We'll take a short break now. I request that everyone who has already auditioned and anyone just here to watch please leave to help avoid distractions."

Hunter walked around Brittany to reach the steps down from the stage, but she caught his arm and engaged him in conversation.

"Yeah, she got the memo now," Savannah said. "And that's why she's throwing half the audience out."

"Which won't help her be alone with Hunter," Jillian pointed out. "He's done with his audition."

Savannah chuckled. "Don't count on it. But I don't think you have anything to worry about. By now, Hunter Greyson has definitely learned how to deal with unwanted female attention."

As long as it is *unwanted.* Jillian felt guilty as soon as the thought went through her head. Of course it was unwanted. Hunter was completely trustworthy. Jillian had once been engaged to a man who was as far from trustworthy as anyone could be, even going so far as to embezzle from his employer, and that had left Jillian a little skeptical of men for a while. But now she was certain Hunter was a good man.

Up on the stage, Hunter peeled Brittany's hand from his arm and then trotted down the steps from the stage. Jillian rose and slipped out of the row to meet him, with Savannah directly behind her.

"Well," Hunter said as he grabbed Jillian's hand. "That was interesting."

"I'll say," Savannah chimed in.

"You were wonderful," Jillian said. "I'm so proud of you for auditioning. I'd be scared to death."

"It helped to have you in the audience," he said. "Would you like to go get some lunch? There's something I've been wanting to ask you about." When Jillian glanced at Savannah, Hunter quickly added, "You should come too, Savannah."

"No, thank you," Savannah said. "I packed a lunch. I knew this was going to be a long day."

"Should I come back?" Jillian asked. "Aunt Cornelia doesn't seem to need my moral support, but I'd be glad to offer it to you."

"No, I'm good. Now that I've seen the auditions in action, I'm surprisingly calm about it." She leaned closer to Jillian. "Not that I expect to get a role. I think James overpraises my singing more than a little."

Jillian returned her attention to Hunter. "In that case, I need to check with Aunt Cornelia, and then I'll be all yours." She headed down the row toward the knot of women listening avidly to something Cornelia was sharing. Jillian hoped it wasn't about her recent flouring, though she knew Cornelia was probably itching to spread that embarrassing story around.

"Oh, there you are," Cornelia said brightly as Jillian reached the group. "This has certainly been more exciting than I expected."

Jillian made a face. "I could have done without the adrenaline rush earlier."

One of the other ladies tittered. "You should be used to that sort of thing. Cornelia tells us that you often go on rather dangerous adventures. I can't imagine."

"I'm usually not seeking out adventure," Jillian assured her.

"Maybe that's been my problem," the woman said. "I seek adventure and never find it. Perhaps if I avoided it, it would come and land on me."

"Like a bag of flour," piped up another woman, making the whole group laugh.

Oh yeah, she told them. Jillian could feel the warmth growing in her cheeks, but she tried to move past it. "Aunt Cornelia, I'm going to have lunch with Hunter. Do you want to come?"

"No thank you," Cornelia said. She waved a hand toward the

adventure-loving woman. "Martha brought a picnic."

Everyone thought ahead but me. Jillian handed Cornelia the keys to the Mustang. "Call me if you need me."

She inadvertently glanced toward the stage and locked eyes with Brittany, who was glaring at her. Jillian felt a chill at the amount of venom in the other woman's expression. *What are you mad about? I'm not chasing* your *boyfriend.* Jillian shrugged and turned pointedly away to walk up the aisle toward Hunter.

"Is there anywhere you'd particularly like to go to lunch?" he asked.

Jillian considered it. She couldn't think of a restaurant close to the theater, and she was considering the surrounding area when her phone rang. "Hold on a sec," she said, answering the call. "Hi Bertie."

Her grandmother wasted no time on pleasantries. "Are you still at the rehearsal?"

"I'm actually on my way to lunch with Hunter," Jillian said. "The rehearsals are on break, but they're probably going to go on all day. Cornelia and Savannah haven't even been on stage yet."

"You're with Hunter?" Bertie's voice warmed with approval. "Where did you run into him?"

"He auditioned." Jillian smiled at Hunter as she spoke. "You should have heard him sing. It was fantastic. I was completely smitten all over again." *And I wasn't the only one.*

Hunter chuckled.

"That's wonderful," Bertie said. "Congratulate him for me. I hate to get in the way of your lunch, but do you think you could come by the bakery? I need you for a second."

Jillian repeated Bertie's request to Hunter, who said, "Tell her we're on our way."

When Hunter pulled into a parking space in front of the bakery, he reached out to take Jillian's hand before she could hop out. "Why don't I go grab some sandwiches from the new sub shop at the end of the street? I can bring them back, and we can eat at the bakery after you do whatever your grandmother needs."

"That sounds great," Jillian said. "I heard the sandwiches there are delicious. Sloppy and indulgent. You have to promise to tell me if I end up with anything stuck in my teeth."

"You have my word on it." He pulled Jillian closer and gave her a quick kiss before letting go of her hand.

Jillian hopped out and trotted to the bakery door. She peered through the glass to see the customer area was packed. Despite the fact that Bertie had insisted Jillian take the day off to accompany Cornelia to the auditions, she still felt a pang of guilt and hoped her grandmother wasn't too buried in work without her help.

She pushed open the door and was greeted by a chorus of welcomes from customers. The friendliness warmed her heart, reminding her again of why she really did love her hometown, even though it was often more than a little loony.

As she slipped behind the counter, Maggie caught her arm. "You'd better hurry to the back," Maggie murmured. "Your grandmother is really annoyed with you."

"With me?" Jillian had no idea what she could have done. She slipped through the doorway into the kitchen, expecting to find Bertie waiting with arms crossed. Instead, her grandmother was humming as she dumped chocolate chips in a tall mixing bowl.

Bertie noticed Jillian in the doorway, then leaned to peer behind her. "Is Hunter with you?"

"He went to pick up some sandwiches from the new sub shop," Jillian said. "You needed me?"

Wiping her hands on her apron, Bertie stepped back from the table. "I need you to read an order you took yesterday. Honestly, Jillian, sometimes I think you should have been a doctor. Did you write it with your feet?"

Jillian considered defending herself, but she had to admit that Bertie wasn't the first person to complain about her handwriting, especially when Jillian was in a hurry. "The order from the elementary school?" As she remembered, she had taken the order with the phone wedged between her ear and her shoulder while she rinsed out the coffeepot with her free hand. Maybe Bertie had a point.

"I think that's what it said. Lenora helped me make out that much, but she gave up on the actual items." Bertie retrieved the pile of order slips and sorted through them until she found the offending one. She thrust it at Jillian.

Jillian took the slip and squinted, mostly trying to remember the call since her handwriting could be challenging for her too. "The principal ordered cutout sugar cookies for one of the teacher meetings, but he wants cinnamon sugar on them." She pointed at a squiggle on the page. "I think that's the part about the cinnamon."

"Any special shapes?" Bertie asked, taking the paper back.

"Leaves." She considered her grandmother as Bertie rewrote the request on the slip. Though Bertie had scolded her, she was clearly not really angry. "I thought you'd be grumpier."

"If you knew I wouldn't like the messy order slip, why didn't you fix it?" Bertie asked, her tone still mild.

"I didn't realize it was a mess at the time I wrote it. I meant that I thought you'd be grumpier when I walked back here. Maggie said you were mad at me."

Bertie tutted. "You girls are always overstating my temper. How's Hunter? You two haven't been out on a date for a while."

"We went out last Saturday."

"Which is a full week ago. Honestly, at this rate, you're going to be a spinster forever."

Jillian put her hands on her hips. "No one says 'spinster' anymore, and I'm perfectly happy with my relationship with

Hunter." And that was the truth. Jillian felt that she and Hunter were in a really good place. He'd come to terms, mostly, with her tendency to get overly involved with problems in town, and she'd come to terms, mostly, with the thought of having a mortician and coroner for a significant other.

"You need to nurture that relationship more," Bertie said. "Or someone will nip in and take him away from you."

A mental image of Brittany hanging on every note of Hunter's singing came to mind, which increased Jillian's annoyance. She was not going to give in to jealousy over Brittany Blaine, even if the woman was rich and beautiful and sophisticated and expensively dressed with perfect hair and nails. Jillian gave her head a shake as if to drive out the spurs of jealousy. "Hunter and I are fine." She looked around the kitchen. "Cornelia connected with some of her garden club at the audition, so I'm free to come back to work."

"You can work after you have a nice lunch with Hunter. No hurry." Bertie spun on her heel and headed back to the work area where she'd been making cookies.

I guess our conversation is over. Jillian headed back to the front, intending to help at the counter until Hunter got back.

Maggie grinned at her. "Nice to see you still have a head."

"She let me live because I'm having lunch with Hunter," Jillian whispered.

Maggie laughed. "That would do it."

When Hunter came in carrying a bulging paper sack, he waved at Jillian and headed straight for what had become their table, the one furthest from the bustle—which also meant they were closest to the bathroom. Jillian figured it was a fair trade for a tiny bit of privacy.

"Did you get drinks?" Jillian called to him.

Hunter raised his eyebrows. "Why would I do that when The Chocolate Shoppe Bakery has the best coffee in town?"

"I'll fetch the coffees," Maggie said. "You go join Hunter before Bertie comes out and yells at you for not marrying him right here in front of everyone."

Jillian chuckled at that silly notion and headed around the counter. She couldn't miss a few grins from patrons as she headed to the table. Bertie wasn't the only person in Moss Hollow who enjoyed a little matchmaking.

When she reached Hunter, she tugged open the bag and breathed in the aroma of the warm subs. The scent made her mouth water and her stomach growl. She felt a little guilty that this was her first chance to eat one of the shop's sandwiches since they bought all their bread from The Chocolate Shoppe.

Hunter held out her chair and she shot him a smile as she took her seat. "Thanks for picking up lunch," she said as Hunter sat in the chair across from her. "If they taste as good as they smell, I may pass out from joy."

"Don't worry, I'll catch you."

"I'm lucky to have you."

Hunter grinned. "Don't forget it. I got you Italian beef. Does that sound good, or do you want my turkey?"

Jillian beamed at him, impressed that he remembered her favorite sandwich and that he was chivalrous enough to offer his own. "Beef sounds perfect."

He reached into the bag and handed Jillian her sandwich. He placed the other one in front of himself and opened the wrapping. "I'm starving. I didn't have much breakfast. I'll admit I had some butterflies at the thought of performing, but it was actually fun."

Jillian unfolded the paper from around her sandwich. "Brittany certainly seemed to enjoy your performance."

"She's a little over the top," he said. "But I think the theater will be good for Moss Hollow. If it's the success she hopes, it should bring more outside dollars into town, and everyone benefits from that. In fact, so far the money poured into the renovation has meant work for a number of local contractors and craftsmen."

Jillian nodded, chewing the delicious sandwich piled with flavorful peppers and melted cheese while he talked. After she swallowed, she said, "You seem to have put some thought into this."

"Brittany was quite a cheerleader for it when I talked to her at Food for Less," he said. "Though a lot of thanks would have to go to her father. She told me he bankrolled the whole project. The family is from Upstate New York, where they are apparently quite well off."

Jillian shivered as déjà vu washed over her. Brittany was reminding her more and more of her old high school nemesis, Nadine Belmont. She'd ridden her father's money right over anyone who got in her way too. And she'd gone after Jillian's boyfriend. Like Brittany, Nadine had been beautiful in the way that only money can buy, and she'd ended up with Jillian's beau and much of her self-respect at the time. Of course, years later, Nadine had also ended up murdered with Jillian as a prime suspect, but that was not the kind of thing that happened more than once. Right?

"Jillian?" Hunter said, leaning across the table to catch her attention. "Is everything all right?"

Jillian blinked at him. "Oh, sure. Sorry, just doing a little woolgathering." She forced a smile at Hunter's concerned expression. "So what made her locate her theater here?" she asked. *Yeah, why here? Why you?*

"I asked her that. She said she'd always loved the South and had a property hunter keeping an eye out for the perfect building. So when the town put the mill building up for sale, she jumped on it."

And now she's trying to jump on you. Jillian gave herself another mental shake. She was being silly. There was nothing to worry about.

Nothing at all.

A full week passed before the final cast list was e-mailed to everyone who auditioned, and it seemed to cause as much stir as the play auditions had. Jillian and Bertie were at the bakery when the roles were released, but they didn't have to wait until they got home to find out how Cornelia fared. It seemed everyone who came into the bakery knew and had some commentary on it.

And the discussion didn't end on Saturday. During the meeting of the Southern Sweetie Pies baking club on Sunday afternoon, the topic was all anyone could focus on. To Jillian's surprise, Bertie didn't even try to resist the group's drift away from actually talking about baking. Instead, she simply helped pass out slices of the pie that Savannah had made.

"It's shoofly pie," Savannah said with a twinkle in her eye. "I made it in honor of Brittany Blaine."

Jillian burst out laughing. Leave it to Savannah to turn dessert into an act of friendship and loyalty.

Maudie Honeycutt perched on the edge of her chair and waved her fork as she spoke. "Speaking of that woman, Cornelia, in my opinion, you were robbed."

"Absolutely," Wanda Jean Maplewood chimed in to the surprise of no one in the room. There were few things the two best friends disagreed on. "You are a much better actress than Elizabeth Winston."

Jillian doubted that, as she knew Cornelia mainly excelled at overacting, and she doubted Mrs. Winston ever overdid anything. As president of the Moss Hollow Historical Society, she was the picture of rigid propriety.

"*And* a better singer," Maudie added. She popped a forkful of pie into her mouth.

Jillian took a sip of her coffee to hide her disagreement with that statement. "I didn't see you two at the auditions. What roles were you trying out for?"

Maudie laughed. "We didn't audition. We drove over after lunch when Cornelia texted Wanda Jean about the gunshot."

"Imagine that." Wanda Jean's voice was slightly hushed with scandal. "Shooting a gun in a room full of people. Someone could have been hurt."

Jillian tried to control her grin. Wanda Jean had recently vowed to stop gossiping, but it seemed old habits died hard.

"Or had a heart attack on the spot." Maudie pointed her fork at Laura Lee Zane, who was both an excellent baker and a sheriff's deputy. "Couldn't you arrest that Blaine woman or give her a ticket or something?"

"It was a poorly thought-out stunt," Laura Lee said, her brows drawn in a slight frown as she poked at her slice of pie with her fork. "Not technically illegal, though. If someone had gotten hurt, it would have been different, but no injuries were reported."

Maudie crossed her arms. "It's indicative of the problems with the whole thing—crazy stunts, poor casting choices, and then that Blaine woman clearly making a play for Jillian's man."

Jillian winced. Now that Hunter had gotten the lead role, she suspected it was just the beginning of Brittany's pursuit. At least Hunter wouldn't be singing the songs directly to Brittany since Bree Weston had gotten the romantic female lead. However, none of that was the main problem with what Maudie had said. "Hunter Greyson isn't my man," she said mildly. "He's his own person."

Wanda Jean sniffed. "He'll be Brittany's *person* if you aren't right careful."

"Y'all stop that," Lenora scolded. "Jillian does not need you two trying to make her jealous and miserable. Hunter loves her. We can all see it. He'll stand up fine against some outsider flirting with him."

"Sure he will," Maudie said, but her tone was quieter.

"Maybe if he put a ring on her finger, none of us would wonder so much," Wanda Jean added.

"Can we change the subject, please?" Jillian asked.

"Sure." Maudie regarded Cornelia and asked, "So how are you feeling about getting robbed of your role?"

Cornelia raised her eyebrows. "I wasn't robbed. I look forward to playing the housekeeper. The script says she's a mysterious woman who is more than she seems. I think that sums me up rather well."

"Well, it's nice that you're being a good sport about it." Maudie was clearly a bit disappointed that no one other than Wanda Jean seemed to want to get stirred up with her. "I still say that putting Elizabeth Winston in the role of a snooty old bat is typecasting, plain and simple."

Jillian glanced surreptitiously at her grandmother. Typically, Bertie would be grumbling about the club's refusal to discuss baking, but she was calmly eating her pie. Jillian was almost inclined to take Bertie to the doctor. This wasn't normal.

Savannah's voice pulled Jillian's attention back into the conversation as she addressed Laura Lee. "You should come to rehearsal with me," Savannah said. "Right now, there are only two of us in the maids' chorus. Brittany asked us to find some more women before our first rehearsal on Tuesday. You don't have to learn any lines beyond the songs."

Laura Lee shook her head. "I can't sing. I can't dance. I see no reason for me to go to rehearsal with you."

Savannah scoffed. "I've stood next to you in church. I know you can sing. And I just saw you dancing at the Moss

Holloween costume ball."

Laura Lee held up her hand. "Fine. I can sort of sing and dance, but I'd rather be winged in the line of duty than to do either of those things in front of an audience. You can beg someone else." She pointed down the table. "Why not ask Josi?"

A reference librarian at the Moss Hollow Public Library, Josi Rosenschein was sweet and fantastically good at her job, but she was also the quietest member of the Sweetie Pies. Jillian couldn't begin to picture the demure bookworm singing and dancing on stage.

Josi had clearly heard Laura Lee, as her cheeks flushed bright red.

"Stop that," Savannah scolded. "You're only singling out Josi to divert attention."

Laura Lee shrugged and forked a large bite of pie into her mouth.

Jillian tapped Savannah on the arm to get her attention. "Who is the other maid in the chorus?"

"Amber French."

"The server at Crazy Fish? She's sure to know lots of people. As do you. Why aren't you roping in clients?"

"Who says I'm not?" Savannah asked, her eyes twinkling. "And as long as I have my rope out, why don't you come and be in the chorus? As I remember, you took dance lessons at the same time as me when we were kids."

"And as I remember," Jillian said, "I mainly used dance lessons as an excuse to kick Nadine Belmont." Still, being in the chorus would give her a chance to watch Brittany around Hunter. She could probably learn the steps well enough for an amateur production.

Jillian's weakening resolve must have shown on her face because Savannah clapped her hands. "Great! It'll be so much fun to be in the play together. I'll even drive us to the first rehearsal Tuesday, if you want." Savannah directed her attention down the table toward Annalise Reed. "How about you, Annalise? Want to be in the maids' chorus?"

Annalise put a hand to her chest. "I get short of breath thinking about it. I'll be assisting with some of the promotion since the bank is sponsoring the play and Byron asked me to help, but no dancing or singing for me."

Jillian sat back in her chair and nibbled on the last bit of her pie. She hoped the experience of being in the maids' chorus went as well as Savannah expected, but somehow she didn't think Brittany was going to be excited to see Jillian join the play.

With the rest of Sunday and all day Monday and Tuesday to think about it, Jillian's nerves were strung as tight as piano wire on Tuesday night as she followed Savannah into the theater. She was fairly certain that she'd made a huge mistake. On the ride over, Savannah had barely seemed to notice Jillian's anxiety. She'd practically bounced with excitement as she drove.

Jillian, on the other hand, could barely walk down the carpeted aisle. Her knees wanted to wobble. *What am I doing here?* Adding to Jillian's lack of confidence was the certainty that Brittany would enjoy nothing more than pointing out Jillian's lack of coordination and grace once rehearsal began.

Savannah reached back and grabbed Jillian's hand, then looked at her in surprise. "Your hands are ice-cold."

"Nerves," Jillian said. "You know, maybe I'll wait for you in the car."

Savannah laughed and pulled her along. "You'll be fine. Try not to overthink it. It's going to be fun."

As a root canal, Jillian thought.

They reached the stage, and Jillian checked out the other members of the chorus. She recognized a few faces, and realized some of these girls were young, a few even teenagers. Jillian hoped that she wasn't going to be the worst and creakiest dancer in the bunch.

Brittany marched out onto the stage from the wings with an older woman following in her wake. Jillian noticed that the other woman walked with an odd rocking gait. It wasn't quite a limp, but it suggested that she had some kind of physical problem.

Brittany actually stopped in her tracks when she saw Jillian, her face unreadable. She stood frozen for a moment before shaking off her surprise and walking the rest of the way to the center of the stage. Jillian suspected center stage would always be Brittany's favorite spot.

"I'm delighted to see so many people interested in our maids' chorus," the director said. "We may not be able to use all of you, but I'll leave that to my excellent choreographer, Helene Coren." She waved toward the older woman. "I worked with Helene when I was in New York preparing for my role on Broadway. She's one of the best, and you're all very lucky to work with her. I expect you to give her your greatest effort. Now, I'll let Helene tell you about what you'll be doing."

Brittany stepped slightly aside and gestured Helene forward. The choreographer was probably about fifteen years older than Jillian, with salt-and-pepper hair pulled back severely. The tight bun set off cheekbones that could slice bread, and Jillian suddenly felt like this was going to be less like Zumba class and more like boot camp.

"Thank you all for coming to rehearsal so promptly. I very much admire promptness," Helene said, which seemed to annoy Brittany, though the older woman never turned in her direction. "You will all need to work very hard, but you will be glad of the sweat and strain, as I will be molding you into *dancers*." She said the last word in a kind of reverent hush, adding a dramatic flourish with her hands.

Jillian shifted nervously. She was absolutely certain she was never going to do anything worthy of that hushed word.

The choreographer had them sit on the stage while she led them through a series of warm-ups. As they stretched and strained, Helene talked about the care all dancers must give to their bodies. "Your body is your instrument. You must treat your instrument well if you want it to perform."

As Helene bent over one leg and reached her forehead to her knee, Jillian noted that whatever condition had given the choreographer the odd walking gait hadn't made her less limber. *So what's my excuse?* When Jillian tried the same stretch, her forehead came several inches shy of reaching her knee. She sighed.

After the stretches, Helene called for the group to line up near the back of the stage. "I will show you the basic step progression for the maids' chorus. Anytime you cross the stage for any reason, you will do so with these steps." She darted through the progression so quickly that Jillian almost whimpered. Again, the woman's grace made her odd walking style seem even stranger. Thankfully, Helene then took them through it slowly. "I know it appears complicated at first, but once you master this progression, you will be able to handle movement across the stage even with the props and furniture in place."

As the choreographer talked, Jillian noticed a portion of the stage looked funny, as if the floorboards weren't laid quite right. When Helene paused in her explanation, Jillian pointed toward the stage floor. "Is that a trapdoor?"

Helene flashed her an annoyed expression. "Yes, it is, but it is perfectly safe to dance on. It is locked. It is not used in the play until quite late in the third act, and none of you will be on stage at that time." She paused to give Jillian another quelling frown. "Now, if we are ready, I will start the music. Do not begin dancing until I count you down."

She gestured toward the wings. Jillian spotted Porter, the stage manager, nodding backstage. The music started, and Helene spoke loudly over it, counting so the dancers could identify the beat. It was a nice effort, but it didn't seem to help much. The group of maids stumbled and tripped through the steps. To Jillian's great relief, she wasn't one of the worst dancers. She was pretty bad compared to the more talented of the bunch, but she was definitely not among the most hopeless.

Over and over, Helene stopped the group and sent them to the back of the stage to begin again. Jillian began to doubt they'd ever make it all the way across the stage, but even she could see that, after what felt like hours, they did seem to be improving.

Helene waved for them to keep dancing. "Go right by me," she called. "All the way to the front of the stage. Then stop. I don't want anyone dancing off."

The group danced. Jillian counted the steps in her head, trying to move less robotically. She noticed she was falling behind the line a bit but didn't know how to catch up. One of the teenagers was now in her line of sight, and the girl danced with real skill.

Then the girl reached the trapdoor section of the stage. No one had gotten that far before. She did the little hop that came at the end of the step progression and landed directly on the trapdoor, which sprang open.

The teenager dropped through, screaming.

More screams rang out, this time from the dancers still on the stage who rushed toward the trapdoor. Jillian was afraid some people would get knocked into the abyss as others crowded against them for a better view. She took a deep breath and, in her best Bertie voice, barked out, "Get away from the trapdoor!"

The group moved away so quickly that one woman fell backward onto the stage and was nearly stepped on before her friend hauled her to her feet.

Jillian got between the crowd and the hole in the floor and held up her hands to keep them back. "Savannah, can you see the girl? Can we reach her?"

Savannah peered over the edge carefully. "I see her, but we can't reach her from here. Maybe if there's some rope, we could lower someone down."

"There must be a way down to that level besides through the trapdoor," Jillian said.

"No need for that," Brittany said breezily as she nonchalantly sauntered over to the opening in the stage. "There's a trapdoor lift, like an elevator. I can have Porter push a button, and it'll bring the silly girl back up here."

"No!" Jillian snapped. "If the girl is badly hurt, that could make things worse. We need to get down there and get a better idea of where she landed in relation to the mechanism before we haul her upstairs. And we need medical help." She pointed directly at Brittany. "Tell us how to get down there. And call 911. Now!"

Brittany blinked at her, then narrowed her eyes, clearly not liking anything about Jillian's tone. "I don't know who you think you are—"

Before Brittany could finish her sentence, another woman stepped up. "Now is not the time for this. We need to get down to that girl immediately. I'm a nurse. She could be badly hurt, and the fact that she's not yelling up at us makes me think that's likely. So I'm with her." She jerked a thumb at Jillian. "Tell us how to get down there. Then call 911."

A chorus of agreement came from the other dancers, so Brittany sullenly gave them directions to the lower level. "I don't have my phone on me," she complained, "but I'll go to my office."

"Don't bother," a woman called from the edge of the stage, holding up her phone. "I made the call."

"Okay," Jillian said. "Then let's get down to this girl. Does anyone know her name?"

"Ginger Laughton." This came from another teenager. "I know her from church youth group."

"Thanks." Jillian headed across the stage with Savannah and the nurse following. When they got backstage, Jillian said to the nurse, "I'm Jillian Green by the way."

The nurse smiled, showing off beautiful white teeth. "I know. My uncle, John Taylor, is your family doctor. I'm Lana Taylor."

"Dr. Taylor is terrific," Jillian said. "And if his medical skills rubbed off on you, I'm glad you're here. I'm concerned about Ginger. I hope she's okay."

"Me too," Lana said.

Jillian glanced toward Savannah, surprised by her friend's silence. Savannah's face was lined and pale in the shadowy lighting of the backstage hallways. "Do you know Ginger?" Jillian asked.

Savannah shook her head. "I'm worried. If I'd fallen, I would have been yelling for someone to come get me the whole time. Maybe we could go a little faster?"

"These halls are pretty dark," Lana said. "It won't help Ginger if we can't get to her because we fell and injured ourselves. Especially since there's junk all over the place back here."

That much was certainly true. As they hurried down the hallways, they sometimes had to turn sideways to squeeze by pieces of furniture or step over tools left on the floor. Though the public areas of the theater were lovely, the halls backstage were a mess. Jillian sighed as she sidestepped another obstacle. *Surely there's a prop room for things like stray furniture?*

"Here's a flashlight," Savannah said, grabbing a black flashlight off of a stool as she passed it. "I'll bring it along."

Jillian shot her friend a quick smile. "Good thinking."

Finally, they reached the stairs that led to the area below the stage. They appeared to have been part of the original mill, as the wood was rough and warped, making the steps treacherous in the dim light.

As soon as they reached the bottom, a puff of dust rose from the floor, making Jillian sneeze. The whole area seemed to be one large room. Sturdy wooden supports held up the floor above and made it difficult to get a line of sight in the deep shadows. She could see a faint glow ahead and suspected that it came from the open trapdoor.

Lana pointed toward the glow. "Ginger must be over there." She raised her voice and called into the darkness. "Ginger?"

In response, they heard sound but no words.

"Savannah, now would be a good time for that flashlight," Jillian said.

"Got it." Savannah switched on the flashlight, illuminating the floor in front of them.

The three women hurried as fast as they dared toward the trapdoor's light, which grew steadily brighter as they wove their way between pillars. Considering how cluttered the upper hallways had been, the room they crossed was relatively empty, though dusty. A few piles of rough-sawn wood gave them one more thing to dodge before they reached the pool of light that fell on the stage elevator, which was basically a platform in an open metal framework. Sprawled across the platform was Ginger Laughton.

Lana knelt at her side. "Ginger? Ginger, can you hear me?"

Jillian pulled her gaze from the girl and peered at the square of light above. Faces were lined up around the edge. "Is she all right?" someone shouted.

"Too soon to tell," Jillian replied. "Has the ambulance arrived yet?"

"I don't think so. Should we send someone outside to wait for them?"

"Sounds like a good idea," Jillian called back. She heard the buzz of conversation above her, but her attention was pulled quickly back to the elevator platform when she heard Ginger moan.

Lana was holding the girl's hand, her fingers pressed to Ginger's wrist. Savannah knelt on the other side of the teenager, though her attention was on Lana.

"Is there anything I can do?" Savannah asked.

"We're going to have to immobilize Ginger's arm," Lana said. "I'm pretty sure it's broken. There's still a pulse, so I think if we brace her arm and her neck, we can move her to the center of the elevator platform. That's going to be the best way to get her up to the stage. Can you find some wood scraps I can use?" She sketched out lengths with her hands and Savannah took her flashlight to go find some.

Jillian started to follow Savannah, but Ginger moaned again and moved restlessly.

"Help me keep her still," Lana said. "If she's done any damage to her neck or back, she could make things worse by squirming."

Jillian knelt on the platform next to Ginger and took her other hand.

The teenager's eyes fluttered, then opened. "Ow," she groaned.

"You have a broken arm," Lana said. "I need you to hold still for me, okay?" Ginger tried to turn toward Lana's voice, but the nurse laid a hand on the teen's forehead. "Don't move at all. Not even your neck. You have had a bad fall."

The fuzzy expression on the teen's face sharpened slightly. "I know *that*." At the sound of typical teen attitude, Jillian nearly smiled. Surely that was a good sign.

"Tell me what hurts," Lana said.

"Everything," the teen answered. "Nothing too bad though."

Lana gently pressed on Ginger's fingers and toes, asking the girl if she could feel the pressure. Relief colored the nurse's face when Ginger said she could.

Savannah came back with some scraps of wood. "Will these do?"

Lana nodded. "Yes, thanks. Now keep Ginger still." Lana stripped off her light cardigan and then used a rough edge on the metal platform to help her start a rip in the fabric. Once she had the sweater in strips, she pointed to a thin board nearby. "Jillian, help me slide this under Ginger's upper back. Don't lift her or roll her, though. We have to move slowly."

Jillian was impressed by and grateful for the nurse's efficiency. They soon had the board under Ginger. Lana began securing the teen to it with torn bits of sweater.

"Is there anyone else down here?" Ginger asked, her voice tight from pain.

"No," Jillian said. "We came down as soon as we could. But we had to take the long route. Your route was quicker but too exciting for me."

Ginger forced a tiny smile at Jillian's attempt at humor, then she said, "I saw someone."

"Down here?" Savannah asked.

Ginger started to nod, but the strips tying her head down

stopped her. "Yeah. I think so. I might have fainted from the pain. But when I first fell, I saw someone."

"A man or a woman?" Jillian asked. "Was it someone you recognized?"

"I don't know." Ginger's voice fell to a whisper. "I'm not sure. It was more like movement, as if someone was moving around down here. I didn't get a clear look."

"Okay, I think we have you secure," Lana said. "We're going to inch you to the center of the elevator platform so we can lift you up safely."

"That sounds painful," Ginger protested, her voice sounding a little stronger as alarm kicked in.

"It might be," Lana said. "But we'll be gentle." She directed Jillian and Savannah on where to put their hands. "We only need to move her about a foot. Just keep her neck still."

Jillian swallowed her fear of hurting the teen more and followed Lana's direction. Ginger whimpered as they gently scooted her onto the platform so that the lift could operate without worsening her injuries.

Lana addressed the faces surrounding the opening above. "Jillian, Savannah, and I are going to move clear of the lift. Then I'll yell, and you bring up the elevator, but don't touch Ginger. No one should move her at all until the ambulance arrives. Are you ready?"

"No!" someone shouted down. The voice sounded familiar, and Jillian saw it was Amber French. "None of us knows how to run the trapdoor lift."

"Doesn't Brittany know how it works?" Jillian called.

"She's not here."

Where did she go? Jillian wondered if Brittany was on her way down to them. "How about Porter Logan? He must know."

"He's not here either," Amber said. "It's just the rest of the maids. Hold on, the ambulance is here."

For a few minutes, chaos seemed to reign above them with lots of voices shouting and not much comprehension. Ginger finally yelled, "Is someone going to get me out of here or what?"

"I'm sure they'll sort it out," Jillian said, relieved that Ginger's voice had regained much of its strength.

Ginger harrumphed. "My squad told me not to try out. They said this was going to interfere with cheerleading. And now what am I going to do? I can't cheer with a broken arm."

"You'll heal fast," Lana said soothingly. "It's a closed break, which is great. And if you do what the doctor says, you'll be surprised at how soon you'll be good as new."

"I can't even get out of this basement," Ginger grumbled.

"Hello down there," a man's voice called from above. "I think we've figured out this mechanism. I've been told there's medical personnel down there."

"Yes," Lana said. "I'm a nurse at Nathan County Hospital. I work in the emergency room. I have Ginger secured to a makeshift backboard. You should be able to safely bring the lift up so you can get her. The way down here otherwise is narrow, and I don't think you'd get a stretcher through."

"You'd be amazed at what we can do," the man responded, "but the lift is the best idea. If you're ready, we'll bring her up."

Jillian, Savannah, and Lana stepped back from the platform. "We're clear. Go ahead."

The lift mechanism was surprisingly smooth and quiet as it raised the platform and Ginger up to the stage. The darkness down below became almost absolute as the platform filled the hole above them, allowing only a sliver of light all the way around.

"I guess we take the long way back up," Savannah said as she snapped her flashlight back on.

They picked their way back across the dusty room and up the

steps. Jillian suddenly felt a wave of exhaustion, though she knew it was probably just the crash after the adrenaline burst earlier. "I don't know what we would have done without you," she told Lana.

"You would have simply waited with Ginger until the EMTs arrived," Lana said. "You'd have been fine."

Jillian shivered. "Maybe, but I'm glad we didn't have to find out. This was bad enough."

"You know," Lana said. "I wouldn't take what Ginger said too seriously."

Savannah glanced back. "What she said about what?"

"About seeing someone down here. With the stress and shock from the pain, she would have likely been confused. And with wanting desperately for someone to save her, it's not surprising that she might think she saw a sign of someone, a possible rescuer. It doesn't mean someone was actually down here."

"I'd forgotten she said that," Jillian said. "But I hope it was a mistake. I'd hate to think someone was down here and didn't bother to help a kid."

When they finally reached the stage, it was mostly empty. A few women from the maids' chorus were gathering their things, Amber French among them. She walked over to greet Jillian, Savannah, and Lana.

"You just missed the EMTs leaving," Amber said. "They said you did a great job bracing Ginger."

"Good." Lana pulled up a sleeve to check her watch. "I've got to get home and clean up. It's nearly time for my shift. I'll check in on Ginger while I'm there."

"Send her our best wishes," Amber said. "That was terrifying for me, so I can't imagine how bad it was for the poor kid."

Jillian almost smiled at Amber's reference to the high schooler as a "kid," and wondered how many years Amber had been out of the school. By the waitress's youthful appearance,

Jillian assumed it wasn't many.

"Where did Brittany go?" Savannah asked in annoyance. "I can't believe she didn't stay to make sure Ginger was all right."

"She said it was obvious that she was in good hands with a nurse and all." Amber nodded at their shared expression of contempt. "Yeah, we all thought she was an unfeeling monster too. She told us she had things to do, and then called off the rest of rehearsal, as if we were going to try dancing after that." She rolled her eyes. "She did say there would still be a Thursday night rehearsal for the maids."

"Did Helene leave too?" Jillian asked.

"I'm guessing so. I didn't see anyone backstage. I don't know where the stage manager went either." Amber shrugged and hefted her bag onto her shoulder. "I have to run. I don't work tonight, but I think I'm going home to a bubble bath."

"I wish I was," Lana said. "I'll walk out with you."

The two started across the stage toward the front steps.

"I'm going to see if I can track down Brittany or anyone else who works here," Jillian said to Savannah. "I want to talk to them."

"I'll come too." Savannah's mouth quirked into a smile. "Especially since I can't exactly drive off and leave you."

"Oh, right." Jillian offered a rueful smile in return. "Do you need to go? I guess we could just leave."

Savannah laughed. "Don't worry. I'm as eager to talk to that woman as you are. Let's go find her. At the very least, we should tell her that Ginger survived, since she didn't bother to stay and find out for herself."

They headed backstage and back into the narrow halls. Now that they weren't following the specific directions to find the lower stairs, Jillian paid more attention to her surroundings. They found a number of unmarked doors and opened each one, peeking in to check for Brittany. Behind one door, they found a storage closet packed with cleaning fluids, buckets, mops, and brooms. A few other doors led to what appeared to be dressing rooms.

"I hope she's planning to put signs on the doors eventually," Jillian said, "or the play is going to be a chaotic mess backstage."

"I imagine she must intend to," Savannah agreed. Since the hallways had lights, though dim and widely spaced, she wasn't bothering with her flashlight. As a result, they had to keep a careful eye out as they walked to avoid tripping over or bumping into something in their path.

"I still wonder why this junk isn't in a prop room," Jillian grumbled as she squeezed past a folded stepladder.

"Maybe we could ask Brittany when we find her."

"After we finish yelling at her for being heartless?"

Savannah stopped in her tracks ahead of Jillian, nearly resulting in a collision. Jillian opened her mouth to say as much, but Savannah lifted a finger to her lips. "Listen," she whispered.

Jillian listened. Up ahead, she heard someone speaking angrily. She and Savannah crept forward until they recognized the slightly scratchy voice of the choreographer, Helene Coren. The older woman raised her voice still louder, and it became clear she was speaking from behind the door ahead of them.

"You can't fool me," Helene snapped. "I know you unlocked that trapdoor purposely to injure me. Well, you won't get rid of me that easily!"

Jillian and Savannah exchanged glances. Before either could speak, the door burst open. Helene rushed out, only to stop suddenly when she saw Jillian and Savannah. "What are you two doing?"

"We're looking for Brittany," Jillian said.

"To update her on Ginger's condition," Savannah added. "She has a broken arm, but she was pretty feisty when we finally got her an elevator ride up to the stage. I think she's going to be all right."

Helene's tight expression softened. "Thank you for telling me.

I'm so glad the poor child wasn't injured worse. I feel responsible after telling you the trapdoor was safe." Then her face darkened again. "It should have been safe."

"Yes, it should have been," Jillian said. "Do you think the unlocked trapdoor was something other than an accident?"

"I don't want to talk about it." Helene put a hand to her temple. "It's all very upsetting. I need to go." She squeezed by Jillian and Savannah and strode down the hallway, once again displaying the limp Jillian had noticed earlier.

"Do you know where Brittany is?" Jillian called after her, but the older woman paid her no attention and simply disappeared around a corner.

"I'm betting she's in there," Savannah whispered, pointing at the still-open door ahead.

They walked into the mostly empty dressing room. No one was there. They poked around behind some folding screens and stacks of chairs, but as far as they could see, the room only had the one door.

"Was she shouting in an empty room?" Jillian asked aloud.

"Curiouser and curiouser," Savannah said. "I'm beginning to think we've fallen down the rabbit hole, Alice."

Yes, but this isn't exactly Wonderland. Jillian's gaze swept the room once more. Exactly what was going on at the Horse Ridge Theater?

A fter their strange encounter with the choreographer, Jillian and Savannah wandered the backstage halls searching for Brittany. Several minutes passed with no sign of her, or anyone else for that matter, so they gave up.

"Let's get out of here," Jillian said irritably. "If Brittany doesn't care about a person being injured in her theater, I don't know why we're putting so much time into finding her."

Always the voice of reason, Savannah said, "It's possible she cared more than we think. She could have called the hospital to check on Ginger. Maybe she even went to the hospital to see how she's doing."

"I suppose." Jillian made a real effort to shake out the tension in her shoulders. "I'm feeling grimy and grumpy, so I think I'll go home to take a shower and see if some chocolate might be lurking around the kitchen to cheer me up."

Savannah grinned. "Living with Bertie and Cornelia, that's a virtual certainty. I'd ask if I can come along since your house is sure to have better chocolate than mine, but I really should go do some work." A respected accountant, Savannah managed the books of many Moss Hollow businesses.

Jillian continued down the crowded hallway they were in, hoping they were going in the right direction to get out of the maze. "Now I feel lazy. Not lazy enough to give up the chocolate plan, but still lazy."

They soon found themselves in a narrow hall that dumped them out in the lobby. "That doesn't seem wise," Jillian said as they stepped through. "I'm not sure they should let people go from the lobby directly to the backstage areas out of plain sight."

"I expect they'll keep that door locked on performance days." Savannah waved at someone behind Jillian, who turned and saw that Hunter was heading their way from the front doors.

"Hunter!" Jillian said in surprise as he swept her into a hug. "What are you doing here?"

"Rehearsal," he said. "I'll be running through all the songs with Bree. I either beat her here, or she's already inside."

"Is Brittany going to be at the rehearsal?" Jillian asked.

"I hope so," he said. "She is the director, after all. Is there some reason why she wouldn't be?"

"We haven't been able to find her," Savannah said. "There was an accident here earlier we need to talk to her about."

"An accident?" His expression sharpened. "Are you both all right?"

Savannah nodded. "We're fine, just a little dirty. One of the dancers fell through the trapdoor during rehearsal. Fortunately, one of the other dancers was a nurse."

Hunter reached out to pick something from Jillian's hair. "If you didn't fall through, how did you both get dirty?" He glanced toward Savannah.

"We went below the stage with the nurse in case she needed help," Jillian said. "It's really dusty down there."

"Brittany called off the rest of the maids' chorus rehearsal," Savannah said. "Then she disappeared."

"Well, now I don't know what to do." Hunter pulled out his phone and scanned the screen. "I didn't get any kind of alert saying rehearsal was canceled. I'll have to go in and see." He shoved the phone back into his jacket pocket and looked at Jillian. "If you want to stay, we could go for a nice walk afterward. There's something I'd like to discuss with you." Then, as if remembering her friend, he turned his charming smile to Savannah. "You're invited too, naturally."

"Sure," Savannah said. "There's nothing I enjoy more than crashing other people's dates." Before Hunter could protest, she laughed. "It's fine. I actually need to get home and do some work. Plus, it's possible James is missing me."

"Of that, I have no doubt," Hunter said.

With a wave, Savannah left. Jillian watched her friend go, thinking how glad she was that she hadn't lost Savannah to marriage. She could remember other friends who were so consumed by wedded bliss that they cut out everyone else.

"You look pensive," Hunter said.

"Just thinking," Jillian told him. She bumped her shoulder against his. "We'd better go inside so the leading man can get started." She hated to hang around since she felt grubby, but if Hunter welcomed her presence, she also didn't want to leave.

They walked into the theater together. To Jillian's surprise, Brittany stood on the stage. *After all the time we spent hunting for her, she's back to rehearse with Hunter.*

Brittany glared down at Jillian as they walked up to the stage. "This is a closed rehearsal."

"I wasn't sure if you'd ever gotten a report on Ginger's condition." Jillian kept her tone even.

"Ginger?" the other woman snapped.

Jillian narrowed her eyes. "The teenaged girl who dropped through your improperly fastened trapdoor. She's probably going to be fine, though she has a broken arm."

"Yes, I'm looking into how that happened," Brittany said breezily. "Thank you for letting me know. Now you can leave. Rehearsal is about to begin, and it's not a spectator event."

Hunter stepped closer to the stage and spoke in a mild tone. "I'm going to have to insist that Jillian stays. We have plans after rehearsal." Brittany puffed up slightly, clearly ready to protest, but Hunter kept talking. "I understand completely if you can't accommodate that. Sometimes these things don't work out." He offered Brittany a warm smile then. "In that case, I'll simply step down and let someone else take this role. Better to call things off up front before we waste anyone's time." He continued to smile pleasantly while Brittany's face reddened. Then he checked out the stage. "It appears the leading lady is missing too, so I suppose this rehearsal is called off in any event."

Brittany cleared her throat and paused a moment before finally saying, "I suppose your *friend* can stay for rehearsals as long as she sits in the back row. I really cannot allow her to be a distraction. And no phones or recording devices or talking, of course."

Jillian gave her sweetest smile. "Of course."

"As for the other lead actor, I decided the role needed someone with more experience. Bree won't be playing the lead, though I did offer her the role of understudy." Brittany cleared her throat again. "I will be taking the role."

"Are you sure you're up to it?" Jillian asked pleasantly. "You sound a bit hoarse. Perhaps you're coming down with a cold?"

"I'm fine," Brittany said tightly, then pointed into the darkened auditorium. "If you'll take your seat, we can stop wasting time."

Before Jillian could go, Hunter tightened his grip on her hand and leaned over to whisper in her ear. "If you aren't okay with this, we can leave. I don't want any problems between us."

Jillian forced a smile. "I'm fine. Have a good rehearsal." Then she gave him a quick, impulsive kiss. She and Hunter weren't prone to public displays so she felt a little guilty, knowing the kiss was more about staking a claim in front of Brittany than anything else. If Hunter minded, he didn't show it.

Jillian walked through the dim auditorium to the back row, where she was surprised to see Brittany's stage manager standing in the deep shadows at the corner. She gave him a startled smile. "Shouldn't you be down there managing the stage?" she asked him quietly.

Porter shook his head. "Brittany said this rehearsal is to run songs and she could handle it on her own. No special lighting or curtain effects. She doesn't need me."

The last sentence sounded far grimmer than the circumstances seemed to warrant. Jillian raised her eyebrows. "But you're staying to watch?"

"I might need to make some notes for stage direction later," he said, not looking at her.

Jillian noticed the man held nothing to take notes on, but she simply nodded noncommittally and found a seat. So far from the stage, she couldn't hear much of what Brittany said to Hunter, but she watched his face carefully for any sign that he was becoming uncomfortable.

Finally, Hunter began singing, and Brittany joined in on some of the songs. As much as Jillian didn't like the woman, she had to admit that Brittany had a lovely voice and seemed to know how to use it. She also stood entirely too close to Hunter, but Jillian kept reminding herself that Hunter was a grown man and if Brittany got out of line, he could deal with her.

But Hunter didn't seem inclined to deal with her—not even when she coyly put her hand on his arm. Repeatedly.

"Stop being stupid," Jillian whispered fiercely to herself. Then she remembered that she wasn't alone in the back of the room. With her cheeks flaming, she turned to see if the stage manager had noticed her remark.

Porter had stepped slightly out of the shadows and seemed to be focused on the stage with every fiber of his being. His face was dark with unconcealed rage. The intensity of the expression startled Jillian. *Exactly who is he so angry with?* An unbidden thought drifted through her head that anyone with that much rage was a powder keg waiting to explode into violence.

Jillian quickly returned her gaze to the stage, not wanting to get caught staring at Porter. Brittany was practically glued to the front of Hunter's gray suit, her facial expression simpering. Jillian's annoyance at her displays was deepening by the second. With a sigh, she hoped her own facial expression wasn't starting to resemble Porter's.

She risked another quick glance at the stage manager, but he was gone. She squinted into the shadows at the back of the theater, but she didn't see him. Maybe he'd had enough of the rehearsal. She certainly had, though she wasn't inclined to leave Hunter alone with Brittany.

She faced forward again, but her imagination wouldn't leave her alone. Porter had looked murderously angry and then disappeared. It left her with an odd sense of unease, almost foreboding. She rubbed her arms, feeling suddenly chilled.

As the rehearsal wore on, Hunter clearly grew increasingly tired of Brittany's antics. He spent much of the time backing away from her, peeling her hand off his arm, or whispering sternly to her. The woman's body language grew increasingly unhappy until she finally announced the rehearsal was over. "Good work, Hunter," she said, speaking loud enough for the words to carry. "Despite distractions, you're doing great."

"I didn't notice any distractions. Good night." Hunter hurried down the steps from the stage.

Brittany frowned after him. "Don't forget, we'll be having another rehearsal on Friday."

Hunter didn't even glance back, merely raising a hand to wave as he walked. "I'll be there." He practically trotted up the center aisle as Jillian edged out of her row. As soon as he met her, he put his arms around her and gave her a considerably less subdued kiss than the one she'd given him earlier. Jillian had no complaints.

As soon as he released her, she beamed up at him. "You were wonderful. I feel as if I'm seeing a whole new side of you."

"So you're not mad at me?" he asked quietly.

"Why would I be mad at you?"

He sighed. "Our director is not exactly subtle."

Jillian laughed. "I am fairly sure she has never been accused of being subtle. Manipulative maybe, but not subtle. But that's not your fault."

"And you don't want me to quit the play?"

"And deprive Moss Hollow of your performance?" She widened her eyes in mock horror. "I can't even imagine how selfish I would have to be to do that. But I may have to ask for an encore of some of those songs."

He grinned down at her. "For you, anytime." He launched into the most intimate of the love songs from the musical, and Jillian felt her cheeks heat up.

She reached up and put a hand to his lips. "Okay, now you're making me blush. We should go."

He took her hand, and they headed toward the doors leading out of the darkened theater. The second they got to the door, Jillian heard an odd sound from the stage area. Suddenly worried that the trapdoor had opened again, she spun around. The stage was empty. Everything looked fine.

"Something's wrong?" Hunter asked.

"I thought I heard something." Jillian chuckled. "I think I've spent too many hours today wandering around in a dark, spooky theater. It's making my imagination run away with me."

"Then we'd best get you out of here." He pulled her hand up to rest on the crook of his arm, then they walked out into the brightly lit lobby. With the shadows dispelled, Jillian laughed inwardly at her own foolishness. She had nothing to worry about.

Nothing at all.

The alarm going off on Wednesday morning actually made Jillian whimper. There were many things she loved about the bakery, but the early hours weren't one of them. "It's not morning if it's still dark," she'd grumbled many times, but it didn't impress the alarm clock much, and it seemed to impress her grandmother even less.

"The bakery sweetens the day of every person who comes in," Bertie had told her more than once. "So it's our job to have what they need when they need it."

"They could need it a little later," Jillian muttered to her memory as she shuffled into the bathroom. She looked at herself in the mirror. Her wild red curls had taken on a life of their own and stuck out in every direction. She pressed them down, but they sprang back up with far more energy than any other part of her could manage. *I need to cut out late nights when I have to get up so early.*

As she stepped into the shower, she realized Hunter had never said anything special to her after the rehearsal. Hadn't he said he had something he wanted to discuss with her? Maybe he just wanted to pick her brain again about the materials he was using on the old house he was renovating as a hobby. *Nothing earth-shattering, sure, but still . . .*

She sighed as guilt washed over her along with the hot water. She probably hadn't really given him a chance to ask anything. Her annoyance with Brittany had taken hold of her mouth more than once. No wonder he hadn't wanted to bring up anything important.

By the time she came down to breakfast, Jillian was vowing to turn over a new, jealousy-free leaf. She didn't care how much Brittany flirted with Hunter, he could handle it, and she could smile and trust him. She was sure of it.

Bertie glanced up as she shuffled into the kitchen. "Did I hear Hunter's voice last night? Were you two up to anything special?"

"Not really, just rehearsal," Jillian said. "He insisted on walking me in. Hunter Greyson is one of the last true gentlemen."

"I'm glad you appreciate it," Bertie said. "Your grandfather was always a gentleman, opening doors and insisting on carrying things for me. It drove me crazy. Now, I wish I'd shown him more gratitude for it."

"He knew you appreciated him," Jillian said. "He told me once that you just wanted to carve out an independent place where you could be yourself."

Bertie paused in the middle of buttering her toast. "He never told me that."

Jillian picked up her own slice of toast. "But you know he loved you."

"And I loved him. Still do." Bertie went back to buttering her bread briskly, switching topics. "I heard the dance rehearsal ended in catastrophe. I'm surprised it wasn't you that fell through the trapdoor. Glad, but surprised."

"I wasn't dancing fast enough for it to have been me," Jillian said. "I'm pretty certain you're not going to see any of the dancers step on that thing on opening night."

"Sounds wise."

At that moment, Cornelia swept into the kitchen, still wearing her robe. She held Possum in her arms, and the cat's sleepy expression sharpened as he caught the scent of bacon.

Bertie pointed her butter knife toward Cornelia. "Keep Possum out of the bacon."

"That's unkind," Cornelia said. "You know how Raymond loves bacon."

Jillian winced inwardly. She was never going to get used to her aunt's delusion that the slightly chubby cat channeled the spirit of Jillian's great-uncle.

"I know the vet says you give *Possum* too many treats," Bertie replied.

Cornelia settled Possum on the floor next to the table and slipped into her chair. She laid her hands on the tabletop in front of her. "I got a message from Raymond last night."

"A message?" Jillian ignored the glare Bertie shot her and blithely bit into her buttered toast.

"Yes." Cornelia narrowed her eyes. "Danger is coming. Great danger. And death. I would have called you, but I know that Brittany doesn't allow phones on during rehearsals. She's very committed to her art."

Jillian snorted. The most she'd seen of Brittany's "commitment" was a dedication to stealing Jillian's boyfriend. But she wasn't going to bring that up at the table. She'd never hear the end of it. "So, how did you get this message?"

"Do you have to encourage her?" Bertie demanded. No one even looked in her direction, and she chomped her toast in annoyance.

"There was a luna moth in the house," Cornelia said, "which, as everyone knows, is a death omen. Then Possum killed it. That's when I knew he's trying to protect us from the coming danger."

"That cat kills and eats more bugs than a praying mantis," Jillian argued. "I seriously doubt any of them are a message."

Cornelia sighed theatrically. "You were much more open to the supernatural when you were a child."

"When I was a child, you told me ghost stories until I couldn't sleep at night," Jillian said evenly. "If I'd stayed that open, I'd have died from exhaustion."

Cornelia sniffed. "I was merely sharing the history of Belle Haven."

Jillian rolled her eyes, then realized she was mirroring an expression Ginger had made and wondered how the teen was feeling. "Did you hear about Ginger Laughton? Do you know how she's doing?" She knew her great-aunt made it a point to stay as connected as possible to the Moss Hollow gossip network.

"She didn't even have to stay overnight at the hospital," Cornelia said. "But her parents are considering suing Brittany Blaine for negligence over the trapdoor."

"Judging by how much money she must have put into the renovation of that theater, Brittany must be very well-off," Jillian said.

"Or seriously in debt," Bertie suggested. "We live in a plantation-era mansion. Someone could easily think we're well-off. Looks can be deceiving."

"Possibly," Jillian said. "But if so, she's put a lot of money into that deception. The outfit she was wearing last night cost more than most of my wardrobe combined."

Bertie waved a hand. "Appearance is expensive. And the need to keep up appearances has gotten people into serious financial trouble many times. It's something to keep in mind."

From there, Cornelia brought up some people Jillian didn't know and the scandalous amount they'd paid to put in a swimming pool—something not easy to do in Moss Hollow, as it was difficult to dig without striking water. Jillian tuned out the conversation, her mind still on Brittany. Was the young woman really what she appeared to be?

By the time they got to The Chocolate Shoppe, Jillian had finally shaken off the effects of her late night and was glad of it. The bakery was busy from the instant they unlocked the front doors, with Jillian manning the counter since Maggie had the morning off for a dentist appointment.

Jillian wasn't normally a fan of working the front counter, but she realized she was actually enjoying herself as she chatted amiably with Leslie Phipps from the Moss Hollow Chamber of Commerce about an upcoming Main Street beautification project. Leslie was her usual chipper self, but Jillian found it less overwhelming than in the past. She suddenly realized what was making a difference in her morning. It was actually nice talking with customers at the bakery because she wasn't presently the topic of anyone's gossip. That was rare.

Leslie finally wound down and carried her box of doughnuts away, letting Bree Weston step up to the counter. Bree gave the back of Leslie's head an annoyed frown. She leaned across the counter. "That woman could talk the corners off a brick."

"It's possible," Jillian said diplomatically. "What can I get for you today?"

"A poisoned apple," Bree grumbled. "I want to kill a wicked witch."

"We're completely out of poisoned apples. Also, the apple was used against Snow White, not the witch."

"That's right. How did they kill the witch?"

"As I remember, the dwarves drove her off a cliff. Are you gunning for any witch in particular?"

Bree waved off the question. "Forget it. I'm being stupid. I need a dozen muffins for the office, please. Make it a mix."

Jillian began picking muffins out of the display case. "I was sorry to hear you weren't going to be doing the lead in the play."

"Can you believe it?" Bree asked angrily. "I could understand not giving me the role. I tried out like everyone else. I knew I might not get anything. But to give me the lead and then take it back and try to stick me in as an understudy? That's insulting."

"I guess Brittany has missed the stage," Jillian said, though she didn't believe it for a moment. "By the way, your singing was beautiful in the auditions."

"Thank you. I thought I nailed it. Even Hunter said I was fantastic, and you know he's the king of understatement."

"Maybe Brittany decided the female lead should be closer in age to the male lead," Jillian said. "I figure she's around Hunter's age, maybe a little older." She was pretty sure Brittany was a good ten years younger, but she couldn't resist a tiny bit of cattiness.

"You think so?" Bree's eyebrows went up. "I did wonder about those crow's-feet around her eyes."

Now Jillian felt really guilty. She normally didn't indulge in this level of spite.

Luckily, Bree didn't actually need Jillian to comment any more. She was clearly primed to get her frustration off her chest. "I've done musical theater, you know," she said. "I was part of a theater group in college, and everyone said we were one of the best the college had ever seen. Plus, I did a commercial once. It was for the parks department, but it required learning a script. So it's not as if I don't have *any* experience."

Jillian felt like she was standing in a stream of annoyance as Bree's words washed over her. She wondered if that's how she'd sounded to Hunter after last night's rehearsal. If so, it was no wonder he hadn't brought up whatever it was he'd wanted to talk to her about.

She startled slightly as she realized Bree had stopped talking. She handed her the box of muffins.

"Sorry about running on," Bree said quietly, her cheeks reddening. "I guess I was percolating and didn't realize it."

"That's all right." Jillian waved off her apology. "I suspect

Brittany has that effect on a lot of people. You have to let it out somehow."

After Jillian finished ringing up Bree, she looked up at the sound of the bakery door opening. She spotted the sheriff's deputy uniforms even before she could clearly see Laura Lee following behind Deputy Goodman "Gooder" Jones. Jillian had known Gooder since they were young. They tended to still interact like kids, frequently annoying one another, but with a strange affection at the heart of it. Gooder was like the pesky brother she'd never wanted.

But she was still in a good mood, so she waved at the deputies. "Let me guess, Gooder. A bear claw?"

Gooder didn't smile back. "We're actually here on official business. We need to talk to you."

"Me?" Jillian asked, blinking in surprise. "About what?"

"About Brittany Blaine." Gooder pulled a notebook from his pocket. "She's dead."

8

Jillian glanced around the bakery. Every customer gazed at her the way she imagined hungry vultures would eye a sickly wildebeest. *Well, not being the center of gossip was nice while it lasted.*

She focused back on the deputy. "Dead as in the victim of an accident?" she asked. "Or dead as in something worse? I'm assuming we're not talking about a chronic illness. I saw the woman last night, and she didn't seem ill."

Gooder flipped the pages on his notebook. "How did she seem?"

"Flamboyant," Jillian said. "Egotistical. Bossy."

"You didn't like her?"

"Have you met anyone who does?" In her mind, she could hear Bertie scolding her for speaking so ill of a recently deceased woman, but she couldn't help it. Brittany had become a hot-button issue for her in a matter of days.

He didn't answer her question. "Did Ms. Blaine seem worried about anything? Did she act afraid or nervous?"

She mostly acted as if she were after my boyfriend. Jillian decided not to share that thought. That information wouldn't get Gooder out of the bakery any quicker nor diminish their audience's interest. "None of the above," she said. "She is—or, I guess, *was* a very confident person."

"Did you speak to her directly?"

Jillian had to think about that. She wasn't sure she had, other than in her head. "I don't think so. No, wait, I did. I told her about Ginger's injury. A teenager was hurt during an early rehearsal, but you probably know that." She snapped her mouth closed to stop the flow of babble, then waved at the customers milling around the front. "Why don't we go in back to talk about this and I can send someone out to help customers? They shouldn't have to wait around."

"That's all right," Mrs. Meadows called from her place near the pastry display. "I don't mind waiting."

"Me neither," piped up another customer, who smiled brightly at Gooder.

Of course you don't mind. This kind of gossip is prime social currency around here. Jillian folded her arms over her chest. "Is there some reason you came specifically to ask me about Brittany?"

Laura Lee spoke up then, getting a reproving glance from Gooder. "It's not personal, Jillian. We're talking to everyone who had any kind of contact with Brittany yesterday."

"You need to talk to Bree." Mrs. Meadows pointed at the young woman who was lurking near the door. "She was just going on and on about Brittany Blaine. Sounded mad enough to kill, if you ask me."

Gooder and Laura Lee both looked at Bree, and the young woman's face paled instantly. "I-I was just talking," she stammered.

"That's silly," Jillian broke in. "Bree would hardly come in here and rant about Brittany if she'd killed her."

Gooder held up a hand. "No one has said anything about killing anyone. We don't know that Ms. Blaine was murdered. At this point, we simply know she died."

"It looks like she fell," Laura Lee added, getting a fresh glare from Gooder. "Through the trapdoor on the stage. Apparently that also happened to one of the dancers?"

Jillian nodded. She thought of the odd sound she'd heard as she and Hunter were leaving. The stage was empty directly after, but what if it was empty because Brittany had fallen through the trapdoor? What if she was injured, and Jillian could have helped? She was horror-struck at the thought. What if she was partly responsible for Brittany's death?

For a second, Jillian was so lost in her musings that the inquisitive looks of everyone in the bakery faded from her perception. Laura Lee waved her hand in front of Jillian's face, pulling her back to the present. "Can you tell us about the accident you witnessed? Anything you can remember."

"It was during the dance practice for the play's chorus. We're all supposed to be maids. The choreographer, Helene Coren, had us doing this step combination as we crossed the stage. None of us were terribly impressive, but we were getting better." Jillian risked a glance toward Gooder who spun his finger, encouraging her to get on with it. "We'd get part of the way across the stage and the choreographer would stop us, show us the combination again, and restart us at the back of the stage. Finally, she let the group get about halfway across the stage. Some of the younger girls were a little ahead, and Ginger was farthest of all. That's why she was alone when she stepped on the trapdoor."

"And the door gave way?" Laura Lee asked. "Was there any hesitation? Did the door hold for a moment and then give way, or did it open as soon as she stepped on it?"

Jillian looked at her friend in surprise. She hadn't thought to consider that difference. She closed her eyes, trying to remember exactly. When her eyes popped open, she shook her head. "I'm inclined to say it gave way immediately, but honestly I'm not sure. I wasn't watching Ginger closely. I was trying to remember my steps. The girls who were closest to her on the stage might remember better."

"And do you know names of those dancers?" Gooder asked.

Jillian shook her head. "I think I've seen some of the girls in here, but I don't know any of their names. I couldn't even guess their ages for sure. Savannah might know more, or Amber French. They were the two who were recruiting more dancers for the chorus."

"Yeah, I remember that from the Sweetie Pies meeting," Laura Lee said. "We're going to see Savannah after this. When you guys went downstairs, did you see anything that might suggest there was something wrong with the trapdoor mechanism? Any sign of tampering? Any sign of another person down there?"

Jillian shook her head. "It was dusty down there, and dark. I didn't see any fresh signs of anyone being down there. And I'm not sure I would recognize signs of tampering if they were in my face. I'm not exactly handy. Have you checked out the trapdoor?"

"We're looking into everything," Gooder said, his tone guarded. "Did you see anyone argue with Ms. Blaine or show any signs of anger toward her?"

"Bree is mad at her," a customer called from one of the tables. "You should have heard her ranting."

"You already told them that," Bree snapped, then reddened as Gooder and Laura Lee looked her way.

"How much interaction did you have with Ms. Blaine?" Gooder asked Bree.

"Just the auditions," Bree said. "She was a little high-handed, but I didn't think much of it. She had me sing alone, then later she had me sing with Hunter Greyson. When auditions were over, she announced that a list of everyone who got a part would be put out eventually, but she told me I had the part before I left. I was thrilled. I had expected to have to wait until the official casting announcement."

"So what did she do to anger you?" Laura Lee asked.

"She took my part back yesterday." Bree's face darkened, her slim brows drawing together. "I had already called my parents, and my mom had made a big thing of it. She said she was going to have a party and bring a bunch of people to the premiere. I still haven't had the heart to call her back."

"And now you might not have to," Gooder said flatly.

"Now there probably won't be a play at all," Bree pointed out. "That's hardly an improvement. I was mad at Brittany. What she did was unfair and unprofessional, but I didn't want her dead. I just wanted her to give me back the role."

"Did she say why she took it from you?" Laura Lee asked.

"She said she thought it would be better for the role to go to someone with a 'stronger presence.'" Bree's voice dripped with anger.

"But that wasn't the real reason," Mrs. Meadows called out, pulling everyone's attention to her. She gripped her purse primly. "Everyone could see that woman was after Hunter Greyson at the auditions. I think she wanted to make sure he sang all his love songs to her."

Gooder glanced toward Jillian. "Were you aware of this romantic interest in Hunter?"

Jillian bit back a derisive snort. "It was hard to miss."

"How did you feel about that?" he asked.

She rolled her eyes before she could stop herself. "I was thrilled, of course. It's so flattering to have another woman chase after the guy I'm dating. Really compliments my taste." She raised her eyebrows. "That's kind of a stupid question, don't you think?"

"That's a lot of hostility," Gooder replied. "So you were jealous?"

She folded her arms over her chest. "I didn't like or trust Brittany, but I didn't have anything to fear from her. I trust Hunter."

Gooder turned back to Mrs. Meadows. "Did she seem to be *after* anyone else?"

"Not that I saw," Mrs. Meadows said. "But I couldn't say for sure. I might not have noticed. I'm not a busybody."

I'd hate to see your definition of a busybody then, Jillian thought. "You might want to talk to the stage manager, Porter Logan. I think he was in some kind of relationship with Brittany, or maybe he had been or just wanted to be. He definitely didn't enjoy her flirting with Hunter."

"Something the two of you had in common," Gooder said.

"The only thing we had in common," Jillian said. "The man wasn't overly friendly, but he did seem to be obsessed with Brittany." She described seeing Porter lurking in the dark during Hunter's rehearsal and the look of rage on the man's face.

"And that anger was directed at Ms. Blaine?" Gooder asked.

"I couldn't say for sure," Jillian said. "Brittany was standing very close to Hunter, so it was hard to tell which of them Porter was looking at. But I don't remember ever seeing someone so mad."

"So let me make sure I have a complete list of folks who hated Ms. Blaine," Gooder said, pulling his normal drawl out like warm taffy. "You two and this stage manager, Porter Logan."

"There might be one more," Jillian said. "After Ginger was injured, Savannah and I went looking for Brittany to update her on the girl's condition. We couldn't find her, but we did overhear Helene Coren shouting at someone."

"Shouting what?" Gooder asked.

"She said she knew the girl's fall wasn't an accident and that the trapdoor malfunction was meant for Helene herself. She said that she wouldn't be gotten rid of that easily."

"And she was talking to Ms. Blaine?" Gooder asked.

"Maybe, but I don't actually know," Jillian said. "As Savannah and I stood in the hallway, Helene came out of the room and stormed past us. We went into the room where she'd been but found it empty."

"Couldn't she have been talking on a cell phone?" Gooder asked.

"I didn't see her carrying a phone, and her outfit didn't appear to have pockets."

"If it wasn't a phone call, maybe the target of Ms. Coren's anger left by another door," Laura Lee suggested.

Jillian shook her head. "Savannah and I looked, but we couldn't find another door to that room. If one exists, it's well-hidden.

Maybe she was practicing for a tongue lashing she planned to give someone. And maybe it didn't go over well. Maybe it even became violent."

"That's an interesting theory," Gooder said, in a tone that suggested he viewed *interesting* as a synonym for *nutty*.

"We will be sure to ask Ms. Coren about it," Laura Lee said firmly.

Jillian was a bit surprised by Laura Lee's tone. Normally she deferred to Gooder when he was present, though she wasn't above sneaking around behind his back to share information with Jillian when she felt it served the cause of justice. But despite Gooder's clear annoyance, Laura Lee definitely wasn't acting like a subordinate.

"Is that all you want to contribute to our investigation?" Gooder asked.

Jillian thought about the sound she'd heard on the stage before she and Hunter left. "When did Brittany die, exactly?"

"We'll have to wait for the coroner's report on that," Gooder said. "And it's not something I'm sharing with you." His eyes narrowed. "Why? Is there something else you have to say?"

Jillian considered it, but she decided not to mention the sound. Hunter hadn't heard it at all, and Jillian hadn't heard it clearly—and she certainly couldn't identify what might have caused it. It easily could have been her imagination. Unless she heard that Brittany's death could have been tied to the sound, she would keep it to herself. "No, though I'll be sure to contact you if I think of something."

Gooder harrumphed. "I don't doubt that for a second." He flipped his notebook closed and started to leave but turned back to the counter. "I'll take a bear claw to go."

A small smile tugged at the corner of Jillian's mouth. *Some things never change.* She made sure to retrieve the best-looking bear claw in the case. She suspected Gooder was in for a lot of frustration in the days ahead, and she hoped he'd remember this one good thing. She handed over the small paper bag, and, with a nod, he stalked from the bakery. Then Jillian grinned at Laura Lee. "You want something?"

Laura Lee shook her head. "I had breakfast. I'd better catch up with him. See you later."

As soon as the door swung shut on Laura Lee, the customers descended on Jillian with questions. No one seemed overly interested in ordering. Glumly, Jillian realized that her shining moment of not being the center of Moss Hollow gossip was definitely over.

When Maggie finally came in to work, Jillian could have hugged her. Instead, she pulled her to the doorway that led to the bakery kitchen. "Are you okay to work?" she asked. *Say yes, please say yes.*

"I'm fine," Maggie said. "It was a loose filling. They barely even had to drill." She reached up to touch her lip. "Though my face still feels a little funny."

"Just don't eat anything. I've bitten my lip really hard because I couldn't feel it."

"I'll be careful." Maggie glanced over Jillian's shoulder at the full customer area. "It's kind of late in the morning to be this busy on a Wednesday."

"Most of them aren't interested in baked goods, so be sure to make it clear that we're a bakery, not a gossip exchange."

Maggie laughed. "You sounded exactly like Bertie for a second there. I heard about how that pushy woman from the theater was murdered. My dental hygienist said that you were totally justified in killing her, considering she was hitting on Hunter."

Jillian groaned. "I didn't kill anyone, and Gooder said they don't even know that she was murdered."

"I told them you didn't kill anyone," Maggie said, a teasing sparkle in her eye. "I said if you were ever to start murdering people, it would probably be family."

"Are you two done shooting the breeze?" Bertie asked as she walked up to the doorway. "We have plenty of orders to fill and it looks as if you have plenty of customers to serve, Maggie." Before Maggie could dart out into the customer area, Bertie's gaze softened slightly. "How are you feeling?"

"I'm fine," Maggie assured her. "I'll get right to work."

Jillian grabbed an apron and slipped it over her head. The kitchen aprons were anything but decorative. They were long, white, and canvas, though most boasted a stain or two that could never be completely bleached out. They flapped against Jillian's knees as she walked, but considering the alternative was to watch her clothes slowly morph into a collection of icing blobs and flour, she was fine with the aprons. The pink hairnets, on the other hand, she loathed. Bertie insisted on them, though, so she wrestled one over her wild red curls.

She'd barely gotten all the wayward bits tucked under the hairnet when Maggie poked her head back into the kitchen. "Hunter is here for you, Jillian."

Jillian glanced toward her grandmother.

"Well, go on," Bertie said. "Don't keep him waiting."

Jillian honestly suspected that no amount of orders would ever keep Bertie from sending Jillian hurrying whenever Hunter showed up. Bertie had mentally penciled Hunter in as her future grandson-in-law since before Jillian had even come back home to Moss Hollow, and she made no effort to hide that fact.

"I'll be quick," Jillian promised.

"No need. Take all the time you want."

Jillian swept the hairnet from her head. She may have been dating Hunter for a while, but there were some things she tried very hard not to let him see. Her wearing a hairnet was at the top of the list. She left the apron on and walked out to the front. Hunter greeted her with a smile.

"I hoped you could take a quick coffee break with me," he said.

"I can think of nothing I would rather do. Let me grab the coffees." Jillian noticed the customers watching Hunter. Half seemed to be eagerly waiting for some kind of drama, while the others simply beamed at him. *Hunter Greyson has to be one of the most well-liked funeral home directors on the planet.* Of course, he was charming and patient and kind, so that helped.

When she carried the foam cups to the table, she passed by more grins and winks. Briefly, she thought wistfully of the days when she lived in California and no one showed the slightest interest in her. That had been a lonely and stressful life, but there were advantages.

Hunter hopped up to pull the chair out for her.

"You know I can operate my own chair," she said with a smile.

"I'm old school," he said. "You'll just have to live with that."

"I suppose there are worse things." She settled into her seat.

"I heard you had some excitement in here earlier," he said before taking a sip of his coffee.

Jillian smirked. "Sacrificing my privacy seems to be the price I paid for readmission to Moss Hollow."

"People mean well. Mostly."

"Mostly." She took a deep breath and blew it out. "To be honest, I actually feel kind of guilty."

"About what?"

"I met Brittany. I spoke with her. I know loss of life is always sad, but I really didn't like her, and I'm struggling to grieve her."

"I suspect she was a difficult woman to like," Hunter said. "And possibly an even harder one to trust."

Jillian raised her brows. "You know something I don't?"

He took another sip of coffee, making Jillian wonder if he was just delaying his answer. "I didn't appreciate the thing with Bree. This play is a big deal in Moss Hollow, and it was an even bigger deal to Bree." His smile took on a self-deprecating twist. "It was even a big deal to me. The disappointment of getting the lead and having it pulled away must have been awful. Especially since she hadn't done anything wrong."

Jillian set her coffee on the table. "I imagine there are going to be a lot of terribly disappointed people now. Without Brittany Blaine, there definitely won't be a show."

"We could put it on." Gordon Sprague had walked up while Jillian was talking. He stood a barely polite distance away, watching them with an earnest expression. "The town could do it," Gordon continued. "We have the scripts and sheet music, and there are people here who have experience in theater."

"That's up to Brittany's family," Hunter said. "She wrote the script, so I imagine the play belongs to her heir, whoever that is—certainly someone in the family. And the building belongs to the family as well."

"It used to be town property," Gordon insisted. "The town could buy it back."

"With what?" a voice boomed from near the bakery door. Jillian jumped and twisted in her seat to see Mayor Blackwater standing at the entrance. The big man had clearly heard at least the last bit of Gordon's conversation. "That building was sold for a song because it was a nearly worthless property the town had been stuck with for years. But with all the renovations that the Blaine woman did, her family isn't going to let us have it back nearly so cheaply."

Gordon shoved his hands in the pockets of his jacket. "I hate to see the play abandoned. It really was going to be great."

Mayor Blackwater snorted. "I assume you had a role."

"A small one," Gordon said. "Lots of people had roles. Lots of people are unhappy. If it turns out Ms. Blaine was murdered, lots of people are going to want to know who did it."

"People would be better off to leave it to the sheriff's department," the mayor said. "Nothing good comes of citizens playing detective." He gave a pointed look at Jillian and then continued on to the front counter with Gordon behind him, still arguing.

Considering she'd helped out the mayor's family when someone was trying to ruin his daughter's wedding, Jillian wasn't sure why he was being so grumpy about her occasional sleuthing now. "I'm perfectly happy for the sheriff's department to handle this. I think that would be best for everyone."

Hunter reached out and put a hand over hers. "I'm glad to hear you say that. I also think this particular mystery should be left to the experts."

Jillian picked up her coffee with her free hand and nodded before sipping it to hide her face—and her doubts. She had enough experience to know how difficult it was for her to stay out of trouble. It wasn't that she went looking for mysteries, but they seemed to drop on her like spiders in a dusty attic.

Hunter let go of her hand and sat back in his chair. "It does seem we'll have some extra time to spend together."

"That's always a plus," Jillian said, brightening. "Hey, you could tell me what you wanted to talk about the other night after rehearsal. I don't think you ever did say."

Hunter smiled and sat up, but anything he was going to say was cut off when Bertie appeared from the kitchen.

"Jillian?" Bertie called. "I hate to rush you, but Lenora wanted to know if you could decorate some cupcakes. The kindergarten teacher will be here to pick them up within the hour."

"I'm on my way." Jillian knew that if Bertie interrupted her time with Hunter, the need must be serious. She squeezed his hand. "Can we table this for later?"

He smiled. "I should get back to work myself."

They stood, and he leaned over the table to kiss her cheek. Jillian watched him walk out of the bakery. Hunter had certainly stepped up the public displays of affection lately. Then she smiled. She didn't mind as much as she'd thought she might.

"Jillian?" Bertie prompted, cutting into her thoughts.

"Coming," Jillian sang out. *At least in the kitchen I won't have to deal with any more gossip.* She realized that cheered her up quite a bit.

For the next week, Jillian caught more than her fair share of skeptical looks from customers, though only a few were brave enough to ask her pointed questions about Brittany and Hunter. Every time one did, Jillian gave the same answer. "Brittany Blaine was putting on a play, and she was acting in it. My relationship with Hunter is real life." And then she would excuse herself and go hide in the kitchen for a while.

The most grumbling came from people who had been cast in the play and now weren't going to get to fulfill their dreams of stardom. Mrs. Winston, who had gotten the role of the wealthy dowager that Cornelia had wanted, actually marched up to Jillian on the street and said, "I hope you're pleased."

"Pleased with what?" Jillian asked, bewildered.

The elderly woman tilted her head back so she could look down her nose. "Putting a stop to the play because of your insecurities over your boyfriend."

"I didn't put a stop to the play," Jillian said. "Brittany's death did that. And I had nothing to do with it. Nothing."

Mrs. Winston narrowed her eyes. "Well, of course you would say that." Then she marched off.

Jillian watched her go and wondered if Moss Hollow really had an unusually high percentage of crazy people or if it only seemed that way.

On Thursday afternoon, Jillian was cleaning up the cake-decorating area after finishing the last project of the day. As she washed smears of pink and orange from the stainless steel table, Maggie stepped through the doorway into the kitchen. "Can someone with more authority than me come out here, please?"

Jillian glanced over at Bertie. Her grandmother was pounding a mound of rye dough with her fist to fill a large last-minute order for the sandwich shop.

"You handle it, Jillian," Bertie said without hesitation.

Jillian followed Maggie out front, wondering what kind of catastrophe awaited her. To her surprise, she found herself face-to-face with a smiling woman she'd never seen before. The newcomer was young and almost painfully thin with a head of black curls and huge, round glasses that gave her small face the look of a cheerful goldfish.

"May I help you?" Jillian asked.

The young woman held up a stack of papers. "Do you mind if I put one of these in the window?" She held up a handbill, waving it a bit, which made it unreadable.

Jillian gave Maggie a quick, quizzical glance. Maggie knew the shop allowed community postings within a specific area of the front window. *Why would this be something I have to handle?*

Jillian took the brightly printed flyer and read it, her eyes widening in shock. The paper announced that the play would be continuing under the leadership of a new director, and that all rehearsals would resume according to the original schedule after a cast meeting at the theater on Friday night.

Jillian made eye contact with the eager young woman. "This may be a little unseemly." However, even as the words came from her mouth, she knew that a lot of people were going to be thrilled.

"How do you mean?" the young lady asked.

"Brittany Blaine has barely been dead for a week," Jillian said. "The police haven't even released a statement about whether her death was an accident or murder, though hopefully they've told the family. I'm not even sure they've released the body."

"They haven't," the woman said. "But that doesn't have

anything to do with this." She waved the stack of handbills. "The show must go on."

"I'm not entirely sure it must," Jillian said, though she doubted anyone would be interested in her view on the situation. "Do you know who the new director will be?"

"Me!" The woman adjusted her glasses on her nose with one finger. "And my mother is the producer. I'm Melody Blaine. Brittany was my sister."

"Oh." Jillian studied Melody, looking for any speck of resemblance between her and her sister. She couldn't find any. "I'm very sorry for your loss."

"Thank you." The woman held up the stack of handbills again. "May I put one in the window?"

"Sure." Jillian walked over to the window and removed a flyer advertising a high school booster club meeting that had taken place a couple days before. "Just put it right there."

"Thanks!" Melody fumbled in her pocket and produced a roll of tape, then secured the paper to the glass.

As she walked back to the kitchen, Jillian mused that Melody Blaine was either an amazing actress herself, or she wasn't exactly in mourning for her sister.

It didn't take long for the new flyers to get the town buzzing, and few people complained about the lack of respect for the dead. Most were happy to take up their dreams of stardom again, Aunt Cornelia among them.

When Jillian got home Thursday night, Cornelia greeted her in the foyer. "I can't believe you didn't call to tell me."

Jillian shrugged out of her jacket. "Tell you what?"

"About the play," Cornelia said. "I had to go to the Clip & Curl to hear that it was on again."

"You probably enjoyed hearing it more there," Jillian said. "The Clip & Curl is the only place in Moss Hollow with more gossips per square inch than the bakery. Weren't you at the salon recently?"

Cornelia waved off the remark and pulled a handful of paper slips from her cardigan pocket. "I go once a week to pick up new tear-out cards. You know that."

Jillian looked at the papers ruefully. Her great-aunt had once misheard a conversation about tarot cards and then decided to try connecting to the spirit realm with her own collection of subscription cards harvested from magazines all over town. Jillian was surprised that no one had enlightened her great-aunt on her mistake. She certainly never intended to do so. Cornelia definitely didn't need to be messing with real tarot cards.

"Jillian," Cornelia snapped, making Jillian jump. "Are you listening to me?"

"Yes ma'am," Jillian said. "You heard about the play being back on at the Clip & Curl. Since everyone there knows everything, have you heard whether Brittany's death is murder or accident?"

"Murder, silly," Cornelia said. "We all appreciate that Brittany brought theater to Moss Hollow, and we'll always have gratitude toward her for that, but she really was a rather unpleasant young woman. I'm not surprised someone offed her."

Jillian gave her aunt a truly horrified look. "*Offed* her? Where did you get that?"

"Detective shows on television," Cornelia said. "You seem to find yourself in the middle of the most sordid murders. I'm doing research so I can help you whenever one comes along."

"Did someone at the salon say that Brittany was definitely

murdered?" Jillian asked, deciding to skip the lecture about the insensitive term. "Based on what evidence?"

Cornelia wrinkled her nose at the question. "How should I know?" A sparkle lit her eyes. "I wonder if the new director is going to keep all the casting. It's possible she'll see how much more suited I am to the larger role of the wealthy dowager." She waved her handful of subscription cards. "I believe I will go and see what the tear-out cards have to say."

Jillian watched her great-aunt disappear up the sweeping staircase. Her stomach growled, and she realized she was due for some supper.

She found Bertie in the kitchen. Her grandmother had beaten her home after Jillian stopped to deliver some cookies to the public library for a community meeting.

Jillian pointed at the pot Bertie was stirring. "Is there enough of whatever that is for two?"

Bertie nodded. "Tomato basil soup from the freezer. There's plenty if you want to whip up some grilled cheese sandwiches to go with it."

"Sounds like a perfect comfort-food supper. I remember that soup from when you made it. It was fantastic." Jillian opened the refrigerator to retrieve butter and cheese.

"It freezes well too," Bertie said.

"Has Aunt Cornelia eaten?" Jillian asked as she poked around the fridge to see if there was anything interesting she might add to the grilled cheese. She grabbed a small container of leftover caramelized onions. "Should I make three sandwiches?"

"You'd better. I don't know if she's eaten. All she can talk about is the musical." Bertie sighed. "I have to say, I'm uncomfortable with anyone from this family being part of the play. It's ghoulish to continue after that young woman's death, and possibly dangerous."

"You worry too much," Cornelia said from the doorway. "The

play will help bring the community together."

Bertie huffed. "This community is together entirely too often. Besides, I thought you were the one full of dire warnings based on Possum's eating habits."

"You scoff, but clearly Raymond was trying to warn us about poor Brittany's passing," Cornelia said. "Now that the dire event has happened, it should all be fine now."

As she buttered whole wheat bread, Jillian hoped her great-aunt's optimism was valid.

"Are you coming to the meeting tomorrow night, Jillian?" Cornelia asked.

"I wasn't planning on it," Jillian said. "Unless you need a ride. I'm not in the play. My dancing experience in the maids' chorus has me convinced they would be better off without me." She placed the first sandwich on the hot griddle, enjoying the sound of the sizzle.

"I don't much care for driving after dark," Cornelia admitted. "Though I suppose I could ride with Savannah. She's a dear girl. She'd come get me."

Bertie took the pot of soup off the stove and set it on a trivet before turning toward Jillian and gesturing with the soup spoon. "I think you should go. You don't want to go back on your word."

"My word?" Jillian echoed, freezing in the middle of flipping a sandwich over.

"Well, you went to a rehearsal, that was a display of commitment," Bertie continued. "And I don't want anyone saying that my granddaughter isn't as good as her word. You should stay in the chorus."

Jillian felt a little dizzy from Bertie's abrupt about-face. "Weren't you *just* saying you wished none of your family was in the play?"

"Yes, I did say that. But it's not going to happen, is it? Cornelia isn't going to quit the play." She raised her eyebrows at her sister.

"Are you?"

"Heavens no," Cornelia said. "Theater is in my blood."

"Then you should both stay in." Bertie gave Jillian a pointed look and Jillian finally realized that her grandmother wanted her to go and watch after Cornelia.

Jillian pressed a sandwich with the back of her spatula and sighed. "Then I guess I'll be a maid."

Cornelia clapped her hands. "Wonderful. This is going to be such fun."

As Jillian slid the first sandwich onto a plate, she hoped again that her great-aunt's staunch optimism wasn't misplaced.

On Friday night, Jillian and Cornelia arrived at the theater to find it even more crowded than it had been on the day of the auditions. *Surely not all of these people have a part?* Jillian realized that the mystery of Brittany's death had drawn more than a few rubberneckers, which shouldn't have been unexpected. The unpleasant young woman had made herself into a minor celebrity in the town, and now everyone wanted to see the theater where she'd met her end.

I suppose that means ticket sales for the play should be good. As they started down the wide theater aisle, Jillian said, "I guess we should have left earlier. I don't know if we're going to be able to find seats together."

"I have to look my best," Cornelia insisted. She had switched outfits three times before agreeing to leave Belle Haven. "I may be changing roles." Then Cornelia's face lit up. "Look, there's Savannah."

Savannah was standing in a row not far from the front and

waving her arms. Hunter stood up from a seat in the same row and added a wave of his own. Jillian and Cornelia slipped through the crush to find that Savannah and Hunter had saved two seats for them.

"How did you know I'd be here?" Jillian asked as she scooted into the row.

"You're a maid, aren't you?" Savannah winked. "Besides, how could you resist discovering details of a possible murder mystery?"

Jillian saw Hunter cringe slightly at Savannah's words, but Cornelia clearly agreed with Savannah. "You may have to solve the murder," her great-aunt said. "Otherwise, this theater could end up haunted by Brittany's ghost. Theaters are very prone to hauntings. Everyone knows that."

After they settled into their seats, Hunter leaned forward to speak to the three women. "I'm certain the sheriff's department will handle any necessary investigation. For all we know, they've discovered the poor woman was simply the victim of an unfortunate accident."

Jillian nodded. She agreed with Hunter, though she did watch his expression. As much as she wasn't interested in being involved in a police investigation, she also had no desire to see a return of Hunter Greyson's overprotective side. It had strained their relationship in the past.

Hunter saw her watching him, smiled, and squeezed her hand. Jillian felt a wash of happiness at being there with him and any thoughts of murder mysteries were swept away.

All the chatter and rustling in the audience ceased suddenly, and Jillian faced the stage, expecting to see Melody Blaine. Instead, a tall woman in a fawn-colored suit and shockingly high heels walked to the center of the stage with the same sense of her own importance that Brittany had always had.

The woman had silver-white hair worn close to her head

and a sharp nose. "I am Astoria Blaine," she announced, pausing for a moment as if to let the import of her name sink in. "You all met my late stepdaughter, I assume. I am here to ensure that her show continues and succeeds, if only so the family can recoup some of the money Brittany frittered away on her little hobby." Astoria's already severe expression darkened to a scowl as she swept her gaze across the audience. "This play *will* make money. And I expect each of you to do your part to make that happen."

From the quiet grumbling around her, Jillian knew she wasn't the only one who found the woman's tone offensive.

Astoria continued to scowl across the audience without speaking and the muttering grew louder. A male voice shouted from the back of the room. "So, who's going to be the director? You?"

"My other stepdaughter, Melody, will fill that role," Astoria said. "But I am the one taking on the organizational mantle and giving you all this wonderful opportunity. For a small town like this, having a prestigious New York family like the Blaines investing in you is an incredible honor. Everyone will be expected to promote the play and sell tickets." More rustling and grumbles met her remarks, but Astoria didn't leave any time for more questions. "And now I will turn the proceedings over to Melody," she concluded coldly. "She will be the person you will work with directly."

With that, Astoria Blaine spun on her very expensive heels and stalked across the stage. Melody hurried to take her place, a clipboard clutched against her chest. She looked excited enough to vibrate to pieces right in front of them. "Thank you for coming," she chirped to the crowd. "I'm overwhelmed by the reception. All of you are wonderful. My family really appreciates it."

Jillian seriously doubted Melody's stepmother appreciated anything about Moss Hollow, but she noticed that much of the grumbling settled as the young woman's bubbly tone helped soothe the audience's ruffled feathers.

"I won't be making any changes in the cast, though I will be looking for a few people to be stagehands," Melody said. Then her smile slipped. "Of course, I will give the lead back to Bree Weston." Jillian heard a whoop and twisted to see Bree slap a hand over her own mouth, though she was clearly grinning behind it.

Melody's expression cleared, and she gestured toward the side of the stage opposite where her stepmother had disappeared. "Both Helene Coren, our choreographer, and Porter Logan, our stage manager, will be staying on as well."

Jillian looked toward the edge of the stage where Helene watched the young woman sullenly while Porter stared intently at a clipboard of his own and didn't glance up. Even with his head dipped, Jillian could see the man's red eyes. *He must be taking Brittany's death hard.* In a way, it was nice to see that someone felt bad about the woman's passing.

As much as Jillian had loathed Brittany, she found herself feeling increasing sympathy for her. It was clear that her own family couldn't manage the smallest display of mourning. How awful it would be to leave so little in the wake of your death.

Jillian tightened her grip on Hunter's hand, suddenly very, very glad to be herself.

10

All day Saturday as she made bread dough and sugar cookies, Jillian went back and forth in her head about going to rehearsal for the maids' chorus. She really didn't want to dance in front of an audience, though the one rehearsal she'd attended had suggested she might be able to manage it without totally humiliating herself. It was nearly lunchtime when her grandmother noticed how quiet she was.

Bertie carried the order list to the table where Jillian was rolling out cookies. "What's up with you today? Do you feel all right?"

"I'm trying to decide about being in the play."

Bertie set the clipboard of orders on the table. "You'll be in the play. I want you there to watch over your great-aunt. You know that."

"But Cornelia's rehearsals aren't even on the same night as mine, so now I'm going twice a week." Jillian set the rolling pin aside. "It's silly."

Bertie folded her arms over her chest. "Go. It'll be good for you to be part of something the whole town is so excited about. And it gives you more opportunities to spend time with Hunter." She pointed at the basket of cookie cutters. "Do leaves. We got another order for fall leaves."

"Fine." Jillian rooted in the basket for the cutters.

"Fine, you'll use the leaf cutters, or fine, you'll go to the rehearsals?"

Jillian held up a maple leaf cutter. "Both. But if I fall down or throw up on stage, I'm blaming you."

"That seems fair."

It also seemed increasingly probable. As Jillian drove to the theater that evening, her stomach felt distinctly uneasy as she thought about the performance. "That's weeks away," she scolded herself aloud. "And the play may be canceled by then." As pep talks went, she knew hers was weak, but it was the best she could manage.

After working until closing at the bakery, she'd rushed through a light dinner and a shower, but she was still a little late for rehearsal. She doubted the choreographer would be thrilled with that—a thought that made her stomach twist again.

As she walked into the theater, she found the stage already full of women in athletic wear going through the stretches Helene had taught them at the first rehearsal. Thankfully, the choreographer herself was nowhere in sight. Jillian trotted down the aisle, stripping off her jacket as she walked.

When she reached the stage, she realized the woman next to Savannah was Laura Lee. She almost hadn't recognized the deputy without her signature ponytail. Instead, she'd wrapped her straight blonde hair into a bun. Jillian waved and took a spot on the other side of Savannah.

As she began stretching, Jillian whispered, "How did you get Laura Lee to change her mind about dancing?"

"I didn't," Savannah whispered back. "I was as surprised as you. And I haven't had a chance to talk to her."

Jillian leaned forward to see past Savannah but she couldn't catch Laura Lee's eye. Her friend's gaze stayed on the wings, so Jillian turned to see what had her attention. She spotted the choreographer talking to the stage manager. Neither seemed happy. Finally, Helene nodded to Porter and walked out onto the stage, her steps quick even with her characteristic rocking movement.

Helene clapped her hands twice for attention. "Now that you are warmed up and loose, we will see how much you remember. I doubt any of you have practiced since last I saw you."

Jillian certainly hadn't, but when they went through the combination, she was surprised to find she remembered it considerably better than she had expected. Still, Helene stopped the group each time before they reached the trapdoor. She didn't always scold anyone, and Jillian was beginning to suspect she simply didn't want anyone to step on the door.

"Is the trapdoor safe?" one of the younger dancers asked after the fourth time of being stopped and sent back to the starting point.

Helene gave her an imperious scowl. "Of course." She gestured toward the wings. "Come out here, please, Mr. Logan."

Porter trudged onto the stage, glowering from under lowered brows. "What?"

"Did you check the lock on the trapdoor?"

"Yeah. I checked. Twice," he growled. "It's fine."

Helene narrowed her eyes at him and pointed. "Good. Walk on it."

Porter's head snapped up in surprise, then his expression grew angry. "You think I'm lying?"

"I think my dancers will feel more comfortable if they see the trapdoor is safe," Helene said. "And you are the stage manager. You are the one who guaranteed it. I'm sure you will not mind proving the safety of the mechanism."

Porter didn't answer, but Jillian doubted anyone could miss how much he *did* mind being sent out onto the trapdoor. Still, he went, stomping over until he stood directly in the middle of the door. Several of the dancers gasped when he jumped up and down on the trapdoor, as if that was tempting fate simply too much.

"Thank you," Helene said. "I am sure all the dancers feel much more secure now."

Porter scrutinized the group with an expression that definitely didn't make anyone feel safer, then redirected his ire toward Helene. "Can I get back to my work now?"

"This is part of your work, I believe," Helene said.

"Wasting my time is not in my contract." He spun and stalked off the stage, clearly deciding he didn't actually need Helene's permission to leave.

Helene sent the group to the back of the stage again for another run-through of the steps. This time, she didn't call them to stop when they approached the trapdoor. The dancer who reached that portion of the stage first stumbled a bit as she stepped onto the trapdoor, but it held. The group managed to cross the stage without further incident.

"You are all doing much better than I expected," the choreographer said. "So, I believe we can move on to some slightly more complex exercises." She broke the dancers into two groups. One lined up at the back of the stage, the other at the front.

Helene clapped her hands. "Mr. Logan, please bring the props."

No one appeared from the wings, so Helene called his name again. When he still didn't walk out, she pointed quickly at Jillian and Savannah. "You two, come with me, please."

They walked to an area past the side curtain, where a stack of bowls rested on a stool. Jillian glanced around but saw no sign of Porter. Helene picked up the stack of bowls and counted some out. She pushed the small stack at Jillian. "You, hand these to every other dancer in the row at the back of the stage." Then she handed some to Savannah for the dancers at the front of the stage.

As Jillian and Savannah handed out the bowls, Helene said, "This time, you will dance across the stage, but when you meet another dancer, you will either give a bowl or take a bowl and alter your course by ninety degrees." She frowned at the group. "You do know what ninety degrees is?"

"A quarter turn," Laura Lee called out.

"Yes, good. A quarter turn."

The addition of the bowls and pivots created mild chaos, but by the fourth time they'd tried the exercise, things were definitely going better. Though the steps weren't overly strenuous, Jillian was beginning to feel tired and sweaty.

At last, Helene clapped her hands and called the dancers to return the bowls to her. "You did well. We had no broken crockery, which is quite good. Practice your steps at home, please. When we rehearse again, there will be more props. Good night."

As Helene walked off the stage, the dancers began to gather their things. Some had brought towels to mop sweat from their faces, and Jillian made a mental note to do that next time as she wiped her brow on her forearm. She looked around for Laura Lee, intending to quiz her friend on what she was doing there.

She spotted her at the edge of the stage, slipping into the wings. "Curious," Jillian whispered and trotted over to see what was up. Laura Lee's movements were so obviously meant to be stealthy that Jillian didn't dare call out to her or say anything to Savannah, who was packing up a few feet away. Instead, she followed the young deputy into the shadowy backstage area and then to the corridor beyond.

Laura Lee stopped after several yards, though she didn't look behind her. Her focus was entirely on the hallway ahead.

Jillian caught up, put a hand on her friend's arm and whispered, "What?"

Laura Lee spun on her with a frown and held a finger to her lips, then moved her hand to her ear. Jillian listened. From around the corner, she could hear Helene Coren's voice.

"I'm afraid I didn't sign on for this," the choreographer said.

"But you did," Astoria Blaine responded scornfully, her imperious tone making it easy for Jillian to recognize her. "I have the contract to prove it. I have the lawyers to back it up. You will comply. You will stop whining and do whatever it takes to make this play a success."

The choreographer's reply was unintelligible, but the intonation was hostile.

Astoria laughed coolly. "Your opinion of me is duly noted. If it comforts you, you're not the first to make that observation. You don't have to like me, Ms. Coren. You simply have to do the job you agreed to do."

With a sharp click of high heels on the wood floors of the backstage halls, Astoria strode toward Jillian and Laura Lee too quickly for them to get out of sight. Jillian expected a harsh comment from the tall woman, but Astoria barely glanced at them as she strode past.

Following behind, Helene appeared far less self-assured. If anything, she seemed worn out. Upon seeing Jillian and Laura Lee, she stopped. "Did you need something?"

Thinking fast, Jillian said, "We were wondering about the rehearsal schedule for the maids. You said we'd be practicing with more props. Does that mean we'll be rehearsing more than once a week?"

Helene blinked at the rush of words, but merely said, "We'll meet as a full group again next Friday, but after that, I'll be breaking the maids up into the specific scenes where they'll appear, and you'll be rehearsing with the other actors."

"Thank you," Jillian said. "That's really helpful." She beamed at Laura Lee. "Isn't that helpful? I think she covered all my questions. Did you have anything you wanted answered?"

Laura Lee shook her head. "I just wanted to say how much I'm enjoying working with you."

Helene's face lightened a bit. "Thank you. Your group is clearly working very hard. I appreciate that."

The choreographer nodded and moved past them down the hall. Once again, Jillian wondered at the other woman's gait, but it would be rude to ask about it.

As soon as Helene was out of sight, Jillian grabbed Laura Lee's arm. "Want to tell me what's going on?"

"Maybe I simply love dancing," Laura Lee said evasively.

"As I remember, you said you'd rather be winged in the line of duty than to dance or sing in public."

Laura Lee reached up to begin pulling pins out of her hair. "A woman can change her mind."

"Sure, but that same woman would have to have a good reason." She gently poked Laura Lee's shoulder. "Which is?"

Laura Lee's bun fell into her usual ponytail, and she shook her head, as if checking to see that it swung freely. "Being here wasn't my idea."

Jillian was surprised. "Then whose idea was it?"

"Sheriff Henderson's. I'm working undercover."

"Why?"

Laura Lee blew out a frustrated huff. "There's no point trying to keep it secret in Moss Hollow. The tests are finally back. Brittany Blaine fell through the trapdoor, but the fall didn't kill her. She was murdered."

The accuracy of Laura Lee's prediction about the speed with which secrets spread in Moss Hollow was proven many times over. At church the next morning, Jillian overheard several small clusters of parishioners talking about the murder: how Brittany had been poisoned, and then her body thrown down through the open trapdoor.

Jillian also noticed more than one person giving her sidelong looks and wondered gloomily how long this was going to last.

She was so annoyed by the buzz of gossip that she nearly skipped out on the afternoon Sweetie Pies meeting and stayed home at Belle Haven. Her grandmother, however, thought that was a terrible idea.

"The women of our family do not hide," Bertie insisted as she slapped a plastic container on the kitchen counter next to a cooling rack of cookies.

Jillian snagged a cookie from the rack and sniffed it. It smelled of molasses and spices. "Don't think of it as hiding," she said. "Think of it as stress management." She took a bite that would have earned her a scolding as a child, and might still.

"Manage your stress *at* the meeting." Bertie began stacking the cookies in the container. "Or else you cannot ask any questions about what people said when we get home."

"Speaking of home," Jillian said. "Where is Aunt Cornelia? I haven't had a chance to talk to her since I found out about the murder."

Bertie sniffed. "A good question, since these are her cookies she needed me to pack up for her. She's having lunch with some of the women from the gardening club. She said they were planning their flower beds for next year, but I expect they're simply gossiping."

"Which makes them totally different from the Sweetie Pies," Jillian said wryly. "Is she coming to our meeting?"

Bertie paused in snapping the plastic lid on the container of cookies. "I should hope so. It's her turn to play hostess."

Cornelia did make it to the meeting, but she arrived after everyone else. Jillian and Bertie had rearranged the tables in the customer area of the bakery and made the coffee without her help, and Bertie slipped in a snarky remark about the hostess arriving fashionably late. Cornelia ignored her as only a twin sister can—completely and without the smallest sign of having heard Bertie's voice at all.

Since the group was mostly interested in gossip about the murder, no one rushed to take a seat. Instead, they stood nibbling cookies and chatting. Jillian ducked a couple questions about the play and made it to Cornelia's side. She pulled her great-aunt over to a corner. "I wanted to talk to you."

Cornelia's face was a mask of disappointment. "You're not going to scold me for being a poor hostess too, are you? I made the cookies."

"You did, and they're lovely," Jillian said. "No, I wanted to talk to you about the play. Now that we know Brittany was murdered, I think you and I should both drop out. It's dangerous."

Cornelia gaped at her, finally snapping her mouth shut before reproving Jillian. "That would be terribly unprofessional. I have my reputation to consider."

"And I have mine," Jillian said. "People are already looking at me funny."

"Which isn't surprising. That dreadful woman was clearly after Hunter. It's a wonder you haven't been arrested."

Jillian rolled her eyes. "I haven't been arrested because that's ridiculous. Hunter is a grown man and capable of holding off unwanted attention. He's had enough experience, being Moss Hollow's most eligible bachelor and all."

"I know that," Cornelia said. "But you do have a history of being a tiny bit insecure."

"I don't know what you're talking about."

Before Cornelia could answer, Bertie's voice cut across their conversation. "Can we find our seats, please? This is supposed to be a meeting."

It's too bad Bertie didn't want to be in the play, Jillian mused inwardly. *The woman can certainly project.*

Bertie managed to get everyone seated, but she couldn't keep them off the topic of the murder, though she tried more than once. "This is a baking club," she insisted the third time the conversation drifted in that direction.

"I'm surprised you're being so resistant to discussing the problem," Maudie said. "Jillian must be the prime suspect in this murder. I can't be the only person who sees the obvious similarities between this and that dreadful business with Nadine Belmont when Jillian first moved back."

"This is nothing like Nadine," Jillian argued, though she'd noticed the similarity herself, of course. "I didn't even know Brittany. I'd barely met her. The only similarity between the two is that I didn't kill either woman."

"That and the fact that Brittany wasn't poisoned with a cupcake," Wanda Jean said helpfully. "At least I think she wasn't. Was she?"

Jillian sighed. "I haven't heard how she was poisoned."

Annalise folded her forearms on the table in front of her. "It's too bad Laura Lee isn't here. She could tell us."

"I imagine she was smart enough to realize that," Jillian said. "I'd guess she skipped the meeting to avoid this kind of conversation."

Annalise flapped a hand dismissively. "I think Laura Lee is made of sterner stuff than that. I bet the sheriff told her not to come."

"I doubt that. After all, he sent her to play rehearsals," Savannah said, then clamped a hand over her mouth and gave Jillian an apologetic smile as questions exploded around them.

Jillian shrugged. Laura Lee had said she didn't expect secrets about the case to stay secret.

Bertie slapped both palms down on the table. "I wish everyone would back out of the play. Whoever killed this woman might still be around, and I'd prefer all of you to stay safe." Her gaze swept across Jillian, Cornelia, and Savannah.

"Don't be silly," Cornelia said. "I have complete faith in Jillian's ability to solve the murder in time for the show to open to rousing success."

"I'm not trying to solve the murder," Jillian insisted. "We have a sheriff's department for that."

"Tish-tosh," Cornelia said. "You know they often need your help, and I think they appreciate it deep down."

It must be pretty deep. Jillian tried desperately to change the subject by waving her half-eaten cookie. "These are excellent, Aunt Cornelia. What kind are they?"

"Shoofly," Cornelia said. "They are inspired by the pie Savannah made last week. And that song Hunter sang to Brittany at auditions."

Josi, who hadn't been at auditions, asked, "What song was that?"

"He sang 'Shoo, Fly, Don't Bother Me,'" Cornelia said. "It was very funny considering how obviously Brittany was chasing him."

Jillian had to admit it was funny. It also showed that Hunter could take care of himself around predatory women. She said as much and saw nods all around the group.

"We know Hunter is devoted to you," Wanda Jean said. "But you must realize this whole situation is a bit suspicious."

"No, it isn't," Bertie said. "No one with a lick of sense is going to suspect Jillian. Now, can we talk about whether or not we're going to run a bake sale at the church bazaar? That is, if we can pretend to be a baking club for a bit."

"I think we should sell some of these," Josi said, holding up a cookie. "They are wonderful."

Jillian felt a wash of gratitude as the group reluctantly shifted their focus from Brittany's murder to the bake sale. *Now if it were only that easy to move the whole town to a new topic.*

Unfortunately, Monday morning proved that the rest of the town wasn't done with the topic of murder. Bertie sent Jillian straight to the kitchen as soon as they saw a line of people waiting outside the bakery for the shop to open. "If they want pastries, good," Bertie said. "But if they want to gossip, they should go over to the Clip & Curl."

Lenora hooted. "My cousin will thank you for that. If there is one thing Jasmine loves, it's being seen as the Moss Hollow gossip queen."

Bertie stomped over to attach a huge dough hook to one of the floor mixers that they used for their morning batches of bread. "You'd think some of Jasmine's love of gossip would have worn off, considering she's been the butt of it before."

"Gossip's addicting," Lenora said. "And once you're hooked, it's not easy to go cold turkey."

Jillian wished the whole town could go into gossip rehab as she rolled a huge bin of flour over to the row of mixers so Bertie could begin scooping it in. Then she walked over to the freezer to pull out a couple of cakes. Freezing the cakes made them easier to frost without catching crumbs in the icing, and when they had an order for an elaborate cake, that extra step was essential.

She carried two round chocolate cake layers to the decorating center and started work on a dinosaur-themed birthday cake. She soon found the intricacies of drawing frosting dinosaurs took her mind off the gossips out in the public area of the bakery. The kitchen felt like a sanctuary and Jillian sank into it, feeling herself relax for the first time in days.

She'd barely finished piping an orange brontosaurus when Maggie walked into the kitchen.

"Gooder is out front," she told Jillian quietly. "He says he needs to talk to you."

Jillian groaned. *So much for relaxing.* "Tell him I'll be out as soon as I finish this."

"Tell who?" Bertie demanded from across the room where she was using a bench scraper to hack dough into workable pieces. "Is Hunter here?"

"I wish," Jillian muttered.

"Sorry," Gooder said from the doorway. "It's just me."

Bertie pointed a dough-speckled finger at him. "Goodman, you're not supposed to be back here."

"I need to talk to Jillian," Gooder said. "And I wanted to encourage her along. I know how she can drag her feet when she knows it's me."

"Hardly. Now hush while I write on this cake." Jillian picked up the pastry bag and turned her back to the deputy.

"This is a murder investigation," Gooder said, his tone sharp. "I don't have time to stand around while you draw pictures on cake."

"I'm not drawing the pictures. I'm writing the message. Shush."

Gooder put his hand on his hips. "Jillian, do I have to take you out of here in cuffs?"

"Goodman Jones!" Bertie roared as she stormed across the room to where the deputy stood. "No one is getting handcuffed in my place of business. And if you try that, I'll call your grandmother and tell her how you're behaving toward women these days."

Jillian snuck a glance behind her and saw Gooder hold up both hands, though Bertie didn't even come up to his shoulder. "No one is getting cuffed. But I do need to talk to Jillian."

Bertie folded her arms across her chest and glared at him.

"Fine." Gooder slumped in surrender. "Jillian can come by the office at her convenience. How's that? Can we not call my grandmother?"

"I suppose," Bertie said, though she still fixed him with a baleful eye. "But you'd best run along and do the rest of your investigating elsewhere."

"I will expect to see you soon, Jillian," Gooder said. Then, before Bertie could say anything else, he ducked through the door.

"Why does he want to talk to you?" Bertie demanded as soon as he was out of the kitchen.

Jillian shrugged. "How should I know? I suppose he wants to talk more about my raging jealousy over Hunter. A jealousy which doesn't exist, by the way." *Or at least it isn't raging. Much.*

Bertie sighed. "I suppose you'd best head over to the sheriff's department then. But after you finish the decorating orders. We need to get those done."

"Yes ma'am," Jillian said, then returned to the cake, doubting she'd be able to recapture her earlier peace.

She had plenty of chance to try, but though she decorated two more birthday cakes and a batch of teapot-shaped cookies for a ladies' luncheon, Jillian found that the knot of worry in her stomach never loosened. Why did Gooder want to talk to her? Was it just Brittany's pursuit of Hunter? Surely the sheriff and his deputies knew better than to consider Jillian a real suspect. The questions and thoughts whirled around and around in her head until she finished piping a lacy design on the last cookie and placed it on a rack to let the icing set.

"I'd best head over to the sheriff's office before Gooder comes back," she said to her grandmother.

Bertie gave a noncommittal grunt. "I should have called his grandmother."

Jillian nearly shuddered. Ophelia Jones was scary, and she was no fan of Jillian. "I'd hold off on that. I'll tell you what this is about when I get done."

"Unless they arrest you," Lenora offered cheerfully, then chuckled to herself.

Jillian slipped her apron over her head. "If they do, I'll trust you to bake me a cake with a file in it."

"I'll bake you two," Lenora promised.

When she got to the sheriff's department, Jillian told the woman at the front desk that she was there to see Gooder.

"He told me that you'd find your way in here eventually," the receptionist said drily. "Go on back to the interrogation room. He said you know where that is."

"I do," Jillian admitted, though she shot the woman an annoyed glance. *What's with the attitude?*

She settled in the interrogation room and passed the time texting Savannah, asking her friend if she had any guesses about what Gooder might want.

Why don't you text Laura Lee? Savannah responded. *Wouldn't she know?*

"Probably," Jillian said out loud. But she didn't want to get Laura Lee into trouble if she could avoid it. Granted, she would have appreciated a little forewarning. Laura Lee was usually good for that.

She was still pondering her proper response to Savannah's text when Gooder walked in.

"You took your time," he said, sitting in the chair across the table from her.

"Bertie wouldn't let me out until I finished two cakes and a pan of cookies."

Surprisingly, Gooder smiled. "Reminds me of when we were kids."

"I didn't decorate cakes when we were kids," Jillian said, confused.

Gooder shook his head. "Not that. One time I came over to Belle Haven with my dad. He had to talk to Bertie about something. Anyway, you were there, but she wouldn't let you come outside and play with me until you finished your homework. And as I remember, you didn't get it done before I had to leave."

"I don't remember that, but it definitely sounds like Bertie." Jillian exhaled in a gust. "So, what do you need from me? I'm optimistically assuming I don't need a lawyer."

Gooder raised his eyebrows. "I heard from several people that Brittany was chasing Hunter. And the time of death is shortly after Hunter's last rehearsal with the woman. A rehearsal that you attended, I believe."

Jillian felt a wash of relief at hearing that. "In that case, I definitely have an alibi. I was with Hunter for a couple of hours after that rehearsal, and then back at Belle Haven with Bertie and Aunt Cornelia."

Gooder scribbled in his notepad, then set it on the table in front of him. "So, what do you think about the case?"

Jillian felt her mouth drop open. Though it wasn't unheard of, Gooder was definitely not in the habit of asking Jillian's opinion on cases. "Really? You want to know what I think?"

Gooder folded his hands. "I wouldn't have asked otherwise."

She narrowed her eyes. "Are you feeling all right?"

"If all you can do is be snarky, forget I asked."

Jillian held up a hand. "I'm sorry." She paused to think about all she'd seen at the theater. "There seemed to be a lot of hostility between the choreographer and Brittany."

"Yeah, Laura Lee floated that theory," Gooder said. He picked up his notepad and flipped through the pages. "She was a private dance teacher in New York City, an occupation she took up after injury ended her own stage career. The Blaines are from Upstate New York, but apparently the family spends a lot of time in the city. When Brittany was a teenager, they paid for her to take dance lessons with Helene Coren. Then Brittany hired her to help her prepare for a role in *Beauty and the Beast* on Broadway."

"So Brittany really *was* on Broadway?" Jillian said. "I kind of thought she made that up."

"Don't get too excited," Gooder said. "She was Third Woman Carrying a Bucket, or some such. When I talked to Ms. Coren, she said that Brittany was a terrible dancer, though she had a lovely singing voice. And more importantly, that Brittany's father has very deep pockets."

"Doesn't sound like they were close," Jillian said.

He shook his head. "I think the choreographer mostly wanted to be close to the Blaine money. I got the feeling her job as a dance teacher didn't quite pay the bills in the big city. So when Brittany asked her to come to Moss Hollow and choreograph this play, she came."

Jillian furrowed her brow. "That still doesn't really explain the hostility I saw. It seems as if Helene would be happy to get a payday. Was she worried the family would stiff her?"

"Close. After Helene had signed the contract to be the choreographer, Brittany apparently found someone else with more name recognition and wanted to drop Helene. However, Helene had a contract and she intended to force Brittany to honor it, a fact that made Miss Blaine most unhappy."

"And that's why Helene thought the trapdoor had been rigged on purpose," Jillian said. "I bet she thought Brittany was trying to cut her out of the play."

Gooder closed the notebook. "That's what she said."

"Doesn't that sound a lot like motive?"

"Possibly." Gooder absently flipped the notepad over and over in his hands, and Jillian wondered again why Gooder was being so open about the investigation.

"You know," Jillian said. "I also think the relationship between Brittany and the stage manager was weird. Maybe he was a stalker or her ex or something. I'm not sure. But he had some pretty strong feelings for her."

"He's an odd one all right," Gooder agreed, but he didn't elaborate.

Jillian wondered why. *Does he not know more about the man?* She considered asking but wasn't sure she wanted to burst the unusual bubble of openness. She held out open palms. "So, are we done here?"

"For now. I mostly wanted to hear what you thought."

"Why?" she asked, not able to resist any longer. "This is completely unusual for the deputy I know and butt heads with. What's going on with you?"

Gooder sighed and ran a hand though his short-cropped hair. "I'm in a hurry to solve this one. Half the town is tied up in this play, and I don't want to see violence spill over onto people I know. And the sheriff doesn't want that either. Much as we don't usually like you butting in, I have to admit you've been right a few times."

Ah. Jillian knew Sheriff Henderson could be very convincing when he wanted something. In some ways, he was like Bertie in that. If he was putting pressure on Gooder, Jillian could see that leading to the deputy feeling a little desperate. "I see," she said slowly.

"I doubt that," Gooder replied with a grin. "But please let me know any thoughts you have, no matter how harebrained or nutty."

Jillian frowned. That last part sounded more like the Gooder she knew. "Anything for you, Gooder."

She was still feeling a little unsettled by Gooder's unexpected openness as she walked out of the station. Distracted, she didn't notice the bespectacled young lady right outside the door until the woman approached her.

"You're Jillian Green, right?" Melody Blaine's eyes were red and slightly swollen, and her voice had the faintly nasal sound of a stuffy nose. She was either coming down with something, or she'd been crying.

"Are you all right?" Jillian asked.

Melody sniffled. "I'm fine." She peered past Jillian into the sheriff's department. "I need to go talk to the sheriff about Brittany's murder." She turned back to gaze into Jillian's eyes. "I know who killed my sister. And he's not going to get away with it!"

Since she could hardly head straight back to the bakery after hearing Melody's declaration, Jillian decided to go back into the sheriff's department with her. "Who are you talking about?" she asked as she guided Melody into the reception area.

Melody didn't answer. Instead, she marched up to the front desk and slapped both hands down on the wood. "I demand someone go arrest Porter Logan. *Now.* He just tried to kill my stepmother!"

12

Melody's declaration certainly got things moving. During the chaos, Jillian hung back and watched. Eventually, enough questions were asked and answered to determine that Astoria wasn't in any kind of immediate danger.

Gooder came out to meet Melody with Laura Lee right behind him. "Miss Blaine," he said. "I think it'd be best for you to come back with me."

Melody put her hands on her hips. "More talk? You should be sending someone out to arrest Porter Logan!"

"And I might," Gooder said. "But it will help if you come in and give us a little more information. Calmly."

Melody finally let him cajole her past the reception desk and toward an interrogation room. Jillian wasn't able to slip in, though she did get a nod from Laura Lee. She wasn't completely sure what the nod was meant to communicate. It might have been, "I'll tell you all about this later," but it could also have been, "You'd best go on before Gooder arrests you." That was the trouble with nods.

Either way, it was abundantly clear that she'd get no more information in the outer room of the sheriff's department, so she headed back to the bakery. She arrived to find Hunter standing at the counter, ordering cookies.

Jillian felt the little flush of warmth that still came whenever she saw him. She walked up behind him and put a gentle hand on his back. "I hope they're treating you well here," she said.

"I have no complaints," he said, then leaned down and gave her a quick kiss on the cheek. Jillian heard a titter from behind her at one of the tables and her cheeks grew even warmer. She wondered if her love life would ever stop being of interest to the citizens of Moss Hollow.

"Cookies?" She nodded toward where Maggie was filling a white box. "Do you have a visitation at Greyson & Sons?"

He shook his head. "No, but I do have a meeting with Astoria Blaine and her daughter. They're planning to have Brittany's funeral here in Moss Hollow as soon as her body is released, which is imminent now that cause of death has been officially determined."

Jillian was stunned. "Why would the family bury Brittany here? Wouldn't they take her back to New York?"

"Apparently not," he said. "Though I can't discuss details at this point. There will be an obituary in the paper tomorrow after I get some information from Mrs. Blaine, then you'll know as much as I do."

"All right," Jillian murmured, still trying to sort out why the family would do something so bizarre. Surely Brittany had family and friends in New York that would have wanted to pay their respects. Why bury her so far from home?

She jumped slightly when Hunter put a hand on her arm. "Do you have a moment? I'd love to grab a cup of coffee and chat."

Jillian saw Bertie beaming from the doorway to the kitchen and raised her eyebrows in question. Bertie nodded emphatically and Jillian almost laughed. Bertie was *always* in favor of Jillian spending more time with Hunter.

"Coffee for both of you," Maggie said with a smile, holding out two cups.

"Thank you." Hunter took his cup and picked up the box of cookies. He turned to Jillian. "Shall we? I can finally tell you about the progress I'm making on the Bender Creek house. I've been meaning to update you for weeks now."

"There's nothing I'd enjoy more." Jillian accepted the other cup from Maggie and followed Hunter to their table.

They sat, and he launched into a story about putting wallpaper up in the old farmhouse. He showed her a photo of the progress on his phone, and Jillian was glad to see he'd chosen one of the wallpaper patterns she had liked best when he'd first shared samples with her. She was impressed by his work, though after all the painting and wallpapering she'd done at Belle Haven, she'd never see it as something to do for fun and relaxation. *Better him than me. If I never paper another wall in my life, I'll be happy.*

Finally, Hunter took a sip of his coffee and gazed at her over the rim of the cup. "I have rehearsal tonight. Want to come?"

"Of course," Jillian said, then sighed. "Though I honestly wish none of us were in the play."

Hunter set his cup down and folded his hands. "I thought you'd feel better about the play since Bree will be playing the lead. You two are friends."

"Yes. It was unfair of Brittany to take the part from her," Jillian said, then she realized he was talking about Brittany's interest in him. "I'm concerned about safety, not flirting. Just a little while ago, I was at the sheriff's office and Melody Blaine came in and announced that Porter Logan tried to kill Astoria. Plus, there was the so-called 'accident' with the trapdoor that hurt Ginger, which Helene didn't seem to think was an accident at all. I'm not convinced anyone in the play is really safe."

"Why does Melody think the stage manager tried to kill her mother? Is Mrs. Blaine all right?" Hunter asked. "I have a meeting with them in a couple hours."

Jillian shrugged. "Apparently she's fine, though I didn't get a lot of details before Gooder whisked Melody to the back to question her."

"She could be mistaken," Hunter said carefully.

"Even if she is, someone killed Brittany."

"That's true, but I see no reason why it should mean danger

for anyone else in the play."

Jillian huffed. "Tell that to Ginger Laughton."

Hunter eyed her quietly, his blue eyes serious. "Is this your way of asking me to leave the play?"

"It would be," Jillian said, "if I could get Aunt Cornelia and Savannah and Laura Lee out as well. But if my great-aunt and my friends are going to be in this horrible thing, I guess I'm glad you'll be there to help keep them safe."

Hunter reached across the table and took her hand. "I'll keep them safe. And you too. Unless you're quitting the maids' chorus?"

"I should. I'm definitely not a person who ought to be dancing in front of an audience, but Bertie has informed me that I need to honor my commitment, by which she means she wants me to keep an eye on Aunt Cornelia, even though I won't be with her much outside of the dressing room. And I can be backstage keeping an eye on things when she's on. I couldn't just sit in the audience and fret."

Hunter shook his head. "I don't like the idea of anyone in the audience distracted by worries about safety."

"This is Moss Hollow," Jillian said. "A smart audience should always be worrying."

Hunter chuckled, but before he could say anything else, the door to the bakery opened and Cornelia herself hurried in. She came right to their table. "Thank goodness," she said, taking Jillian's free hand. "I heard you'd been arrested."

"That's ridiculous." Jillian pulled a face. "Where did you hear that?"

"From Jasmine at the Clip & Curl," Cornelia said. "She said Gooder came right into the bakery and nabbed you."

Jillian groaned and Hunter stood. "Sorry to interrupt, but I'm afraid I have to go and prepare for my meeting." He smiled down at Cornelia. "It's always a joy to see you, Cornelia."

"It's always good to see you with my niece," Cornelia said as she slipped into Hunter's seat. "Now tell me about your arrest, Jillian. Are you out on bail?"

Jillian held up a finger indicating for Cornelia to wait, then said to Hunter, "I suppose I'll see you at rehearsal."

"Why don't I come to Belle Haven and pick you up?" he asked.

"Sounds good." She gave him one last rueful smile, then set to the task of explaining to an apprehensive Cornelia that she had never been in danger of arrest.

Thankfully, the rest of Monday managed to be almost normal once Jillian calmed Cornelia down and sent her on her way. It helped that Jillian mostly hid in the back and baked. In the late afternoon, Jillian was scanning the orders for the day, making sure they hadn't missed any, when her grandmother walked over.

"I thought I might go home," Bertie said. "If you don't mind closing."

"I don't mind," Jillian assured her, pleased that her workaholic grandmother was leaving early. "I'm going to play rehearsals later with Hunter, but I should be home in plenty of time for that."

Bertie appraised her critically. "Be sure to leave yourself enough time to clean up. You're a mess. You don't want Hunter to see you too many times in that state."

Jillian gave her a wry smile. "You're very encouraging."

"I think honesty has more value than empty encouragement." Bertie reached up and rubbed at her temple. "But I didn't mean to be critical. I have a wretched headache."

Jillian looked at Bertie in surprise. Her grandmother wasn't usually prone to apologies, and that came awfully close to being one. "You go on then," she said. "I have Lenora and Maggie to help me clean up."

Bertie smiled at her. "Thank you."

As Jillian watched her grandmother leave, she thought of how much had changed since she came back home to Moss Hollow to help with the bakery. All of her work experience had been in advertising, and she'd been hopeless at anything in the kitchen. But now she was confident—well, mostly. She suspected she would panic if she didn't have Lenora around for some of the difficult pastries, but she had all the basics down pat.

She chuckled to herself as she began putting away ingredients and dropping scoops into the sink to wash. She guessed she really was a baker now. *Who'd have thought?*

Monday afternoons were often slower at the bakery and no more orders came in, so Jillian had no trouble finishing the cleanup and was out of the bakery shortly after it closed. She couldn't give up the last shreds of worry about the play, especially with another rehearsal that night, but at least she wouldn't be up on stage. And she did enjoy hearing Hunter sing love songs.

Almost before she knew it, she was sitting in the darkened theater as Hunter and Bree practiced their singing and choreography for their two big romantic scenes. As Hunter clasped hands with Bree and sang, Jillian didn't feel the slightest tingle of jealousy. It wasn't that Bree wasn't pretty. The young woman certainly was. But it was clear that Bree's focus was on doing well in the role, not in specifically finding new reasons to cozy up to Hunter.

"See," she whispered, "I'm not a jealous person." *No,* she added silently. *I'm just a person who talks to herself in a dark theater.* Her phone vibrated in the pocket of her jacket, making her jump. Jillian pulled out the phone, shielding the screen as much as possible to avoid distracting the actors on the stage.

Laura Lee was calling.

Quickly she scrambled out of her seat and whispered into the phone, "Just a sec." Once she was out in the lobby, she spoke up. "Sorry about that. I was in Hunter's rehearsal."

"How's it going?" Laura Lee asked. "Any horrors or histrionics?"

"Only singing and dancing," Jillian said. "Please, tell me you're going to clue me in on Melody's visit to the sheriff's office earlier. Did Porter Logan try to kill Astoria Blaine?"

"Not according to Porter or Astoria," Laura Lee said. "We spoke to both of them, and they insist that Melody is being ridiculous."

"What happened?"

"A minor electrical fire in Astoria's office," Laura Lee said. "It was put out quickly and there was very little damage. When we talked to her, Astoria sounded a bit hoarse. I think there may have been some smoke inhalation, but she refused medical treatment."

"A fire." Jillian sniffed the air in the lobby. "I can't smell any lingering smoke."

"Where are you?"

"The lobby."

"That's a long way from Astoria's office. I expect you'd smell it in the halls. I could this afternoon." Jillian heard some rustling over the line, and then Laura Lee continued, sounding a little like she was reading. "Apparently there was some faulty wiring in an old lamp Astoria was using in her office, which used to be Brittany's. At any rate, the lamp sparked and started a small fire. It began just before Astoria entered the office, and she was able to smother the fire with a thick wool blanket from the love seat in the same office."

"Did she seem worried about it at all?" Jillian asked.

"She said both her stepdaughters were prone to being overly imaginative and dramatic," Laura Lee said. "But she did seem . . . off, somehow. I couldn't put my finger on it, but I'm sure she didn't think Porter Logan was trying to kill her."

"Why blame Porter at all?" Jillian asked.

"He found the lamp for Astoria. It seems the lamp that Brittany always used in that room was missing, so he found Astoria a different lamp, which proved to have a short."

"So it could have been intentional."

"Lots of things could be true but aren't," Laura Lee said. "Melody insists she had seen Porter lurking around Astoria's office, but neither Astoria nor Porter back her up. Both say they have no problem with the other, though I honestly don't think Astoria particularly likes anyone or anything connected to the theater."

"That wouldn't surprise me," Jillian said.

"She said the theater is the worst waste of money her step-daughter ever engaged in. And her tone suggested that was saying something. I don't think there was much love lost between the two."

"Makes you wonder when Astoria got to town."

Laura Lee laughed. "I don't think Astoria Blaine is a likely murderer. I couldn't see her getting directly involved."

"Maybe she hired it out."

"Maybe you read too many mystery novels," Laura Lee said.

"Maybe. Thanks for updating me, by the way. I know you're risking the wrath of Gooder Jones."

"Not this time," Laura Lee said. "Gooder actually seemed in favor of keeping you in the loop during the investigation. I've considered checking him for a fever once or twice."

Jillian realized Laura Lee must not know about the pressure Gooder was getting from the sheriff. She decided to keep Gooder's secret—no use giving him a reason to go back to being his normally grouchy self. "He has been acting oddly agreeable. Which may be the biggest mystery of all." Then she smiled and said, "Maybe he's finally realizing I'm a great investigator."

That made Laura Lee laugh harder than Jillian thought was

completely warranted, and she bid her friend goodbye while the deputy was still chuckling. As she shoved her phone back into her jacket pocket, the doors leading to the audience seats opened and Hunter walked out.

"On break?" Jillian asked.

"All done," he said. "I noticed you left. Was my singing that bad?" Though his tone was teasing, Jillian detected a note of real concern.

She slipped her arm through his and squeezed. "Your singing was wonderful. Maybe you could do an encore in the car on the way home."

He grinned down at her. "As much as you like."

As they strolled through the lobby, Jillian leaned into him. "I had to step out to talk to Laura Lee on the phone. She was telling me about Melody's visit to the sheriff's department and the subsequent investigation. Apparently, it all came to nothing. How did Melody seem to you this evening?"

"She seemed fine. Very competent," he said. "She has a decidedly less hands-on style than her sister."

"For which I am truly grateful," Jillian said.

They stepped out of the theater and into the parking lot, which was dark enough that Jillian was glad of Hunter's arm to keep her from stumbling.

"I hope they're going to put in lights before the actual performance dates," she said. "This isn't really safe. I'll have to make sure Cornelia doesn't come to rehearsals alone."

"That's probably wise." Hunter tugged her to a stop. "Of course, I can't say that I don't enjoy being with you in the moonlight."

"There's not much moonlight tonight."

"That's all right," he said. "I have a vivid imagination."

Though it was actually too dark to see him clearly, Jillian could tell by the sound of his voice that he was bending his head closer to hers. She started to think she didn't really mind the dark parking lot when suddenly a pair of headlights snapped on nearby, dazzling her to blindness.

An engine roared and the lights grew even brighter as a car raced across the lot, heading right for them.

13

Hunter swung Jillian around, dragging them both out of the path of the car so quickly that Jillian couldn't keep up. She stumbled, grateful for the tightness of his grip. The car roared past them, kicking up gravel that drummed against Jillian's legs. Her light-dazzled eyes couldn't pick out any details of the vehicle beyond the fact that it was a car and not a truck.

"Are you all right?" Hunter asked.

She sagged against him. "Yes, thanks to you."

"That driver must have seen us. The lights were blinding." He pulled out his phone and punched numbers.

"Who are you calling?" Jillian asked.

"The sheriff."

She peered up at him in surprise, wishing she could see his face better. The glow from his phone screen gave him a spooky shadowed visage. It was the kind she remembered from childhood sleepovers, when she and Savannah would shine flashlights below their chins and tell ghost stories. She wrapped her arms around herself and shivered, though the night wasn't particularly cool.

Hunter must have felt the shiver since she was still pressed against him, and he led her through the parking lot even while talking on the phone. He unlocked his car, and they both got in. "Do you want me to put on the heat?" he asked.

Jillian shook her head, though she couldn't resist wrapping her arms around herself. "I think it's residual shaking from what happened. Why would someone want to run us over?"

Hunter raised his eyebrows. "Have you been investigating? That seems to be what usually prompts this kind of thing."

"I haven't," Jillian insisted. "My only interest is in keeping my family and friends safe. Maybe the person was texting and driving or something. Maybe it wasn't intentional."

"Maybe, though anyone so distracted as to miss seeing us in those headlights would probably have run into a car."

"There aren't many cars in the lot," Jillian said. "Which might be why a person felt safe roaring out and not taking proper care."

In the interior lights of Hunter's Lexus, Jillian could see his face clearly, and his concern was obvious. He shrugged out of his suit jacket and passed it to Jillian. "You should at least cover up until you feel warm."

She used the suit jacket like a blanket and luxuriated in the residual body heat coming from it.

Hunter launched into a completely unrelated story about growing up in Atlanta. Jillian knew he was trying to distract her and help her calm down. She appreciated the effort, though it was still difficult to follow the rambling story. Her brain kept playing back the headlights snapping on in the darkness and the roar of the car engine.

When Deputy Tom Shaw arrived, he asked minimal questions and, though he carefully recorded their answers, it was clear the lanky, young deputy thought they'd been the victims of an inattentive driver.

"You said the parking lot was very dark, and you're both wearing dark clothes," the deputy said as he wrapped up the interview. "So it's likely the driver didn't see you prior to turning on the headlights, and it would only take a moment of inattention to miss seeing you at all. You'd be surprised at how often that's the core reason for an accident."

"That's possible, I suppose," Hunter said. "But I hope you'll at least speak with anyone who had business at the theater tonight.

This isn't a parking lot where just anyone is likely to park. It had to be someone connected to the theater."

"You had a rehearsal tonight?" the deputy asked.

Hunter nodded. "Yes, with Bree Weston."

"Could it have been Miss Weston's car?"

"I doubt it," Jillian said. "Bree has no reason to try to run us over."

The deputy's tone was mild. "No, but if she were distracted, she still might have been the driver. Since you two were exiting from the rehearsal, it logically might have been her driving." He held up his pen. "Anyone else at the rehearsal?"

"Melody Blaine," Hunter said. "She was running it. I didn't see anyone else, though that doesn't mean there wasn't anyone."

"There was a fire here earlier," Jillian said. "So Astoria Blaine could have been here sorting out her office, and Porter Logan could have been here too."

The deputy frowned. "A fire?"

"Melody was at the sheriff's department earlier and reported it."

"Oh, I hadn't heard."

Jillian stared at him then. How could he not have heard of it? She knew the sheriff's department gossiped as much as the rest of Moss Hollow. "Perhaps you should check into it."

"Perhaps." The deputy closed his notebook. "I think that's all we can do here tonight. You two can go. Drive safely."

Jillian could see Hunter was less than pleased by the deputy's casual dismissal of the near hit-and-run, but he didn't argue.

On the drive home, they were both quiet, caught up in their own thoughts about the evening. Finally, Hunter pulled up in front of Belle Haven. "I'm sorry I wasn't very good company on the drive home. I don't like seeing you endangered."

"I certainly appreciate you saving me." Jillian took his hand. "And though I wouldn't care to repeat the experience, I am definitely glad you were there. I hope it was simply an unintentional accident like Tom believes."

"Me too." Hunter sighed, opening his door. The interior light came on, making Jillian blink and squint. "Let me walk you to the door."

Jillian held up a hand. "No need." She handed him his jacket. "I'm running in and getting a nice hot tea. Unless you want to come in for a cup?"

"I'd like that, but I should get home. I have some busy days ahead preparing for Brittany's funeral."

"Oh, that's right. You had a meeting. How did it go?"

"Fine," he said. "Though the family dynamics there run hot and cold."

"Makes me feel better about my kooky family." She leaned across to give him a quick kiss. "My hero."

He laughed, then kissed her again before she slipped out of the car and trotted into the house. To her surprise, she found Cornelia and Bertie sipping mugs of herbal tea in the kitchen.

"Great minds think alike," Jillian said.

"The kettle is still hot," Bertie said. "How did rehearsal go?"

"Rehearsal was good." Jillian walked around the counter and retrieved a mug and tea bag. "Hunter's singing is amazing."

Cornelia stirred an extra spoonful of honey into her mug. "Well, I'm glad you're still in the play. I'll be rehearsing with the maids on Tuesday."

Jillian poured hot water into her mug. "I wish you weren't. Something creepy is going on at the theater. There have been too many accidents, and I don't think it's safe for any of us."

Bertie's eyes narrowed. "What do you mean too many accidents?"

"Apparently there was a fire in Astoria's office." Jillian sat in an empty chair at the table. "Sounds like it was caused by faulty wiring in an old lamp."

"These things happen." Cornelia took an unhurried sip of her tea.

"And there was the accident with the trapdoor that resulted in a broken arm for poor Ginger Laughton."

"You don't think that was an accident?" Bertie asked.

"The choreographer, Helene Coren, didn't think it was an accident. She thought it was intended for her."

"Vivid imagination," Cornelia scoffed, which nearly made Jillian choke on her own sip of tea. If there was one person who shouldn't point fingers about vivid imaginations, it was Cornelia.

Jillian set her mug down and took a deep breath. "And then someone nearly ran over Hunter and me in the parking lot tonight."

"What?" Cornelia and Bertie exclaimed in unison.

Jillian described the near miss in the parking lot. "I don't think Tom Shaw took it very seriously. He clearly thought it was an accident. Maybe it was, but it felt purposeful."

"I'm very disturbed by this," Cornelia said, laying a palm along her cheek.

Jillian reached out to pat her great-aunt's other hand. "Thank you."

Cornelia blinked at her. "I am glad you and Hunter are all right, but I meant that I'm very disturbed that Raymond didn't warn me about this. Perhaps he didn't tell me because he knew Hunter could take care of you." She shook her head. "I really have to go find Raymond." She drifted out of the kitchen.

"You know, in most families, no one actually converses with the cat," Jillian said. "Or at least they don't think the cat is talking back."

"Don't pick on your aunt," Bertie snapped, surprising Jillian. Bertie was constantly making snide remarks about Cornelia's behavior. Bertie must have seen her expression because she added, "As silly as Cornelia can be, I can totally understand not wanting to let go of the love of your life. I envy Cornelia sometimes. I wish I could believe your grandfather was still with me, even if it was via the cat. You might do well to keep that in mind."

With that, her grandmother bid Jillian good night and headed off to her room, leaving Jillian feeling vaguely guilty and a little confused. What did Bertie mean? She rinsed out all the tea mugs and went upstairs to bed, hoping everything would be more normal in the morning.

The near accident in the parking lot seemed to signal an end to mishaps at the theater, for a few days at least. Perhaps that was because so much attention turned to Brittany's funeral. Rehearsals went on during the week, but much of the gossip among the actors centered on the weirdness of the service being in Moss Hollow.

At the two rehearsals early in the week, Jillian was surprised to see that the initially rather comical efforts of some of Moss Hollow's would-be actors had improved since auditions. She realized it was possible the play might be decent after all. Of course, that didn't mean she couldn't spot tension. It was clear that Melody was desperate for Astoria's approval and not likely to get it. It was clear Porter disliked everyone and everything around him. And it was clear that Helene was jumpy and angry with Astoria. Jillian worried that something was going to give in those relationships eventually, and she wondered if Brittany's funeral might be when that happened.

With that in mind, Jillian felt compelled to attend the service. She hadn't really known Brittany, but the woman had certainly affected Moss Hollow strongly. Still, she had a mild unease about it. Was it respectful to attend a funeral of a woman she had barely known and strongly disliked? She was still undecided on Thursday evening when she found Laura Lee leaning against her Prius in the bakery's back parking lot after work.

"Do you hang out in alleys a lot?" Jillian asked her friend.

"Sure." Her friend grinned at her. "You meet interesting people in alleys."

"I don't doubt it." Jillian stopped beside the car and shoved her hands in her jacket pockets. "Do you need me for something?"

"I wanted to ask if you're going to the funeral tomorrow."

"I was thinking about it," Jillian said. "But I didn't really know Brittany, and I suspect it's going to be something of a gawker's paradise, which isn't the most respectful thing."

"I'd appreciate it if you'd come with me," Laura Lee said. "I don't want to be obvious about watching everyone there, but that's basically what I'm going to do. Sheriff Henderson asked me to go since I have a connection with the play that would explain my presence beyond the investigation."

"So no one will be there in uniform?" Jillian asked.

"Tom will be at the funeral, but mostly he'll be directing traffic. I'm basically the only one on investigative detail, and I could use a second pair of eyes."

"Savannah will probably be there. She could watch too."

Laura Lee nodded slowly. "I'll call her. But how about you? Are you going?"

Jillian sighed. "I can. But I have the feeling it's going to be unpleasant."

"Funerals are always unpleasant."

Since Jillian couldn't refute that, she made plans to meet Laura Lee in the morning and give her a lift to the funeral. She found that she dreaded the whole affair, and the feeling only mounted as the hours passed. She even slept fitfully.

The funeral itself was as crowded as she'd expected. Normally, most people go to the service and then far fewer make it to the graveside, but Jillian actually suspected there were more people in the cemetery itself. Extra gawkers in casual clothes even stood among nearby gravestones.

The whole business left Jillian feeling uneasy. She saw right away that no one standing near Astoria and Melody could possibly be Mr. Blaine. How was it that the man hadn't come to his own daughter's funeral? *How dysfunctional is that family?*

At the graveside ceremony, Jillian, Savannah, and Laura Lee all stood far from one another to cover as much ground as possible while they watched the other attendees. No one seemed particularly sad as far as Jillian could see. She spotted Porter standing some distance from the family. His face reflected the most emotion of anyone, and even he appeared more angry than heartbroken.

Porter's scowl stayed in place as the ceremony finished and the crowd began to disperse. Jillian crept subtly closer to the graveside, hoping to get a better angle for watching Astoria and Melody. She didn't see Helene and wondered if the choreographer had attended.

She was scanning the crowd for Helene when someone poked her hard in the shoulder. "What are you doing here?"

Jillian's attention snapped to the angry man in front of her. Somehow Porter had gotten close without her noticing him, probably because she was so intent on the rest of the crowd. "I'm paying my respects," she said.

"Respects!" A spray of spittle flew as he spoke, and Jillian backed up to avoid it. "There's nothing respectful about you being here. You hated Brittany, and everyone knows it. She wouldn't have wanted you here."

"I did not hate Brittany," Jillian managed to say through her shock at the man's rage. "I barely knew her."

If Porter heard her, his response didn't reflect it. "Everyone was jealous of Brittany. She was so beautiful and good."

Good? Somehow Jillian doubted that was a word that fit the dead woman particularly well. "You knew her better than most," she said gently.

Porter's focus snapped to her. "I did. Everyone thinks she's spoiled and difficult. Only I see how much she needs love and protection. Only I truly love her."

Jillian felt a disquieting ripple at the man's shift to present tense. It was as if he believed Brittany was still alive, even as they stood at her funeral.

"You were a good friend," she tried, unsure of what to say.

At her words, his face crumpled. "I failed her. I should have protected her."

"Protected her from whom?" Jillian asked urgently.

To her shock, the man's rage seemed to flood back. "You have no respect!" he roared, and then he stomped away.

Jillian saw that his yelling had gotten the attention of most of the people nearby, and they all peered in her direction. Most onlookers appeared curious, but Astoria's face was blank, and Melody looked surprised. Had Melody not known about Porter's feelings? What exactly was Brittany's relationship with the stage manager?

Laura Lee walked over. "Well, that was subtle."

"That man is a nut," Jillian grumbled. "I worried for a second that he might hit me."

"You think he might be the killer?" Laura Lee asked.

Jillian shook her head slowly. "He seems torn up that he didn't protect Brittany. I do think he could be dangerous though."

"I wouldn't be surprised." Laura Lee scanned the crowd. "I'll admit, I'd hoped this surveillance would produce some kind of lead. We turned up a nut, but the wrong kind."

"Maybe." Jillian thought that Porter was clearly passionate about Brittany, but he also seemed more than a little unhinged. Could he have killed Brittany and then built up a fantasy about being her protector instead?

14

Rehearsals continued, and there were no more accidents. Jillian actually began to believe that the play might be safe after all. Still, she was disturbed by the lack of progress in finding Brittany's killer. She felt the uncertainty like a pall over each day. Or maybe it was gloom over how little she was seeing of Hunter as rehearsals ramped up even more and his leading role kept him busy every night.

With only a few days left before opening night, Jillian stood in the kitchen at the bakery mixing a batch of chocolate scones and feeling out of sorts. She shut the mixer off when Maggie stepped in from the front.

"We have a customer who wants to talk to my manager," Maggie said. "Can someone please come out and talk to her?" With that, Maggie ducked back into the customer area.

Bertie was opening one of the big ovens to remove fresh loaves of bread baked to golden perfection. "You go," she said. "If someone is picking on Maggie, tell them to shop elsewhere."

"I would," Jillian said, "but I'm in the middle of chocolate scones."

"I'll finish them," Lenora offered. "I'll take mixing scones over dealing with crabby customers every time."

"Thanks, pal," Jillian muttered as she wiped her hands on her apron and headed toward the customer area. She whipped the pink hairnet from her head before passing through the doorway.

A small line stood waiting for service. Jillian could see most of the customers' eyes weren't on the pastries in the display but on the tall, imperious woman standing beside the case. Jillian glanced at Maggie, who nodded toward Astoria Blaine.

"How can I help you, Mrs. Blaine?" Jillian asked.

The other woman sized up Jillian's flour-dusted clothes, putting Jillian in mind of a similar appraisal she'd once gotten from the woman's stepdaughter. "I know you." Astoria narrowed her eyes. "How do I know you?"

"I'm in the play."

Astoria sniffed. "Are you in charge here?"

"I suppose," Jillian said mildly. "Though the bakery belongs to my grandmother."

"I see. Then I will speak with your grandmother. I'm not in the habit of talking to hirelings and stray relatives."

Jillian smiled, inwardly eager to see what Bertie would have to say to the interruption. "Of course. Let me tell my grandmother that you're waiting. May I tell her what you wish to speak to her about?"

"You may not. As I said, I'm not in the habit of talking to hirelings and stray relatives."

Jillian trotted back to the kitchen in a considerably cheerier mood. She knew it didn't reflect that well on her that she enjoyed the idea of Bertie knocking the woman down a few pegs, but she figured she could live with that.

"Astoria Blaine is out there," Jillian told her grandmother. "And she'll only talk to you."

Bertie huffed. "What a nuisance. As if I have nothing better to do." She parked the rolling cart full of fresh bread in a corner, then, not even bothering to remove her hairnet, she marched by Jillian, who followed her out into the customer area.

"Mrs. Blaine," Bertie said, "what can we do for you today?"

Though the words were polite, the tone reflected every bit of Bertie's annoyance, and everyone in the bakery stopped their own discussions to watch the drama unfold.

Astoria narrowed her eyes, obviously not missing Bertie's tone. "I have been told that this bakery does catering."

"We do," Bertie said.

"I have also been told that your pastries are superior to anywhere else around," Astoria continued. "Though I don't expect them to be equal to what we get in New York, I am open to considering your bakery as a caterer for a meeting I will be having at the theater."

"How open-minded of you." Bertie cocked her head slightly. "I still don't see why you didn't simply order something by phone or from either of the two people who have already spoken to you."

Astoria squared her shoulders, her expensive camel-colored wool coat shifting slightly on her willowy frame. "You must be aware of the generosity of my family in restoring that dreadful old mill building. I was hoping the community would show their appreciation for our efforts."

Bertie crossed her arms over her chest. "I imagine they did that by doing such fine restoration work at the breakneck pace your daughter pressed for."

"Brittany was my *step*daughter," Astoria said. "So, you don't feel any responsibility to support the new theater?"

"I will definitely support the new theater. I plan to buy a ticket for opening night to watch the play." Bertie smiled at the customers around them. "I imagine everyone here will."

Astoria gave a pinched smirk. "I was hoping for a bit more, perhaps the donation of some desserts for the meeting? You may include promotional material for your bakery." Her nose wrinkled as if she'd caught a bad smell. "As long as the promotional material is discreet."

She expects free pastries in return for—what? Exposure? Everyone in the area already knows the bakery. Jillian studied Bertie's face to see her response.

Bertie didn't respond. Instead, she simply gave the woman a level stare.

"A local restaurant will be providing the main meal for the meeting," Astoria said when the silence grew uncomfortable. "Crazy Fish is the eccentric name of the place. I hope the seafood is palatable. At any rate, I was told that your desserts are superior to theirs, and since they'll be offering their services for free, I assumed you would as well."

"I find it hard to believe that Malcolm would cater anything for free any more than I would." Bertie held up a finger and pulled her cell phone out of her apron pocket. "Hold on a second while I give him a call."

"That won't be necessary." The angles of Astoria's pinched face seemed to sharpen even further. "I haven't gotten a final agreement from the owner yet. I've only spoken to a hireling." She sighed deeply. "Which is why I loathe talking to hirelings."

Jillian watched Astoria backpedal with interest. She figured that the "hireling" Astoria had spoken to was Amber French, and that the haughty woman had bullied the poor server until the girl had agreed that maybe there was something her boss could do. *Amber's just a waitress. She certainly couldn't promise anything.*

"I'm not going to donate food to a business meeting," Bertie said, her voice dropping in volume to a deceptive quiet that made several customers actually back away from Astoria. Bertie didn't put up with nonsense, and everyone in town knew it. "Community spirit doesn't work that way." Bertie snatched a pamphlet from a nearby holder and slapped it down on the counter in front of Astoria. "This outlines the catering services we offer and the prices. If you want to employ the bakery after considering all your options, feel free to call and place an order with whoever answers the phone. If you decide not to use our business, I am certain there are other options available to you. For example, our local grocery, Food for Less, sells pastries in their bakery department. Now, if you don't mind, I have work to do and orders to fill for paying customers." With that, she spun on her heel and marched back to the kitchen.

Jillian jumped to the side to let Bertie by, but she didn't follow her grandmother. Instead, she watched the fuming woman on the other side of the counter. Clearly, Astoria wasn't used to being refused.

The tall woman's gaze landed on Jillian in the doorway. She pointed directly at her, her arm straight and stiff as if she were acting out the Red Queen's role in *Alice in Wonderland*. "You're out of the play. And I do not expect to see you at the theater again."

And off with my head, Jillian thought in dark amusement.

Astoria whirled and stormed out of the bakery.

Jillian was surprised to find she felt mildly disappointed to be out of the play, especially after all the work and practice she'd put in. At least she wouldn't have to worry about her questionable dancing anymore.

Jillian stayed busy for the rest of the day, though she found her thoughts turning to the play several times. She decided to call Savannah to ask her to keep an eye on Cornelia during the last few rehearsals. Sure, the accidents had stopped, but she'd feel better knowing someone was watching over her great-aunt. Since the maids were in many of the same scenes as Cornelia, Savannah should be able to handle guard duty.

Shortly before closing, Jillian was out front, wiping down empty tables. The bakery door opened and Hunter walked in, beaming at Jillian. "Were you planning to come to rehearsal tonight?" he asked. "And if not, would you consider coming if I tempt you with supper first?"

"I'm not sure that's going to work," Jillian said hesitantly, surprised that Hunter hadn't heard about her firing from the play. The Moss Hollow gossip network was usually more efficient.

"I know we don't have a lot of time," he said. "But I thought we could grab something from Cheap, Cheap Chicken." He winced as he said the name. "I'll owe you a nice dinner. I promise."

Jillian laughed. "You know very well how much I love the Chicken. They use the same family recipe as Lenora, and I am more than Southern enough to admit to loving fried chicken. That's not a problem."

"So can I steal you away? I'll ask Bertie, if you want."

"No need to ask," Bertie called from the doorway to the kitchen. She flapped a hand at Jillian as if shooing her on her way. "You two go on."

Jillian went, though she suspected Bertie was actually looking forward to hearing about the fireworks when Jillian showed up at the theater after being banned. She told Hunter as much as they headed out to his car.

"Banned?" Hunter frowned as he opened the car door for Jillian. "Why would you be banned?"

Jillian stood by the open door for a moment, explaining about Bertie refusing to do free catering for Astoria Blaine.

"If you can't be there, then I won't be there either. You come with me tonight, and if there's anything said, I'll tell them where I stand on the issue."

Jillian pecked his cheek. "My hero, though you'd end up with the whole town mad at you." She slipped into the car. "Unless you have an understudy I don't know about."

"No, I don't," Hunter said brightly, "so Astoria will have to decide if it's more important to have her play go on and showcase the theater, or to continue acting like she owns this town and can strong-arm everyone in it into doing whatever she wants."

After eating, they got to the theater only to discover that Astoria wasn't even there. And it appeared that she hadn't shared her decree with Melody, as her stepdaughter smiled at Jillian when she waved everyone up onto the stage for a meeting before the beginning of rehearsal.

Melody gave them all a pep talk about the upcoming performance and thanked them heartily for all their hard work. "We still have some late nights ahead before the opening night, but I'm so impressed with all of you." Then she clapped her hands and gestured for everyone to join in.

When they quieted, Gordon Sprague raised his hand. "Will your mother be here tonight?" he asked, peering toward the stage wings.

"I doubt it," Melody said, and her tone suggested she hoped not. "My stepmother has a great deal of work to do in her office."

"Oh, so she is here?" Gordon asked, and something about his question got Jillian's sharp attention. *Why is Gordon interested in Astoria's whereabouts? Has he run afoul of the dragon lady as well?*

Gordon must have seen Jillian's curious stare. He leaned closer to her to whisper, "Astoria Blaine is a fascinating woman, don't you think?"

"Sure." Jillian suppressed a smile, remembering Gordon's last big crush. That one had been on Bertie, leading to him spending hours every day at the bakery. The only result of that had been a slight widening of Gordon's waistline from the daily treats. It was clear that he'd moved on. Apparently Gordon had a type: strong women who weren't interested in him.

Melody announced that they were going to try to run through the play from beginning to end. "Anyone not in the first scene can take a seat in the audience. Just move up to the wings in time for your scene."

Jillian joined most of the other cast members in the auditorium. The first scene included only the main actors, including Gordon, who played the butler. She was impressed by how smoothly the rehearsal went, and they made it all the way to the end of the first act before Melody called a break because one of the props was missing. "Don't go far," she told everyone. "We're only taking a quick five."

Jillian met Hunter as he came down the stage and offered him one of the bottles of water they'd bought at Cheap, Cheap Chicken. "Thank you, dear lady," he said with a bow.

"Happy to oblige, kind sir," Jillian answered. "You're doing great."

"Your words kindle in my heart like coals on a hearth," he said, quoting a line from the play.

Again, Jillian laughed. "The lines are a little heavy-handed when you use them in real life."

"Maybe a little," he agreed.

Bree came up to them, offering a hesitant smile. "Sorry to interrupt. Hunter, I had a question about one of the lines."

Jillian gave the young woman a warm smile and backed away while Hunter and Bree discussed the line in question. She walked over to where Savannah and Laura Lee sat and chatted with them until Hunter joined them. Before he could speak, Melody called the actors back to the stage.

"My art awaits," Hunter said, making Jillian laugh again.

She sat down next to her friends and settled back to enjoy the pivotal scene that featured the main characters discovering a dead body. The body was played by an older man Jillian recognized from the church choir but didn't know well. She watched Hunter help the man kneel and lie down on the stage, and she hoped they wouldn't have to rehearse that scene too many times.

The scene began, and each character voiced dismay over

finding a dead body in the middle of the drawing room.

Mrs. Winston played the owner of the house, and she clutched a slightly moth-eaten fur stole around herself. The older woman gave a clear shudder at the pretend corpse. "I do not know this man," she announced, "and I won't have him cluttering up my Persian carpet." She turned toward the wings and snapped, "Jenkins!"

Jillian knew that must be Gordon's cue, as he played the butler, but no one came from the wings. The actors exchanged glances. Mrs. Winston repeated her line, ending by bellowing, "Jenkins!" The woman was impressively loud for someone her age.

Despite the volume of her voice, Gordon didn't appear.

"Where is our butler?" Melody asked, walking from the opposite wing. She shielded her eyes to peer out into the audience. "Could someone go find him?"

"I'll check outside," Laura Lee offered, hopping up.

Jillian stood as well. "I'll go backstage."

Savannah followed Jillian. "I'll keep you company."

"I'd rather you stay and keep an eye on Cornelia." Jillian nodded toward where her great-aunt was sitting with some members of her gardening club who had minor roles in the play.

Savannah nodded. "You got it."

Jillian trotted up the steps to the stage, then headed for the darkened wing that Gordon was clearly meant to have come from. Behind her, Melody told everyone to take another short break.

The shadowy area beyond the curtain was empty of people, so Jillian continued to the door that she knew led to the backstage corridors. She heard footsteps behind her as she walked, and she whirled to find Hunter.

"Sorry," he said. "I didn't mean to startle you. I just don't want you to wander backstage alone."

"I don't much want to do that either."

They walked through the labyrinthine hallways, which were

still cluttered, though not as much as last time Jillian was there. Many of the pieces of furniture had been arranged on stage to make up the drawing room set. Still, there were plenty of other props and chairs to dodge as they wove their way down the hall.

"I bet Gordon went in search of Astoria's office," Jillian whispered to Hunter, though she couldn't have said why she felt the need to whisper.

"Why would he do that?" Hunter asked.

"He's sweet on her."

Hunter gave a single bark of laughter. "That man has interesting tastes."

"I don't suppose you know the way to Astoria's office?" Jillian asked.

He shook his head. "But Gordon probably doesn't either, so he could be wandering back here."

Suddenly Jillian froze, holding up a hand. She had heard something, though she would have been hard-pressed to say exactly what. "Is someone there?" she called out.

She didn't get any response, so she continued forward, dodging around a pile of debris on a narrow table. Then her foot struck something soft, and she would have fallen if Hunter hadn't caught her.

She squinted down to see what she'd stumbled against and gasped. Gordon Sprague lay sprawled on the floor in a disquieting replica of the pretend body on the stage.

Even in the darkness, Jillian could see the blood on his bald head.

Jillian knelt at the retired teacher's side and was grateful to hear Gordon moan. He raised a shaky hand to his head as he tried to sit up. She caught his wrist and said, "You're bleeding a little. It's best not to touch it."

Gordon dropped his hand and used it to lift himself to a sitting position. "You know, getting bashed in the head is becoming entirely too familiar."

Jillian winced. Once before, Gordon had been clobbered by a murderer who was trying to cover up her crimes.

"Someone hit you?" Hunter asked as he knelt beside Jillian.

"I'm not sure." Confusion filled Gordon's face. "I was on my way to Astoria's office. I wanted to speak to her about . . . something."

Jillian sat back a bit and raised an eyebrow. "You do know Astoria is married, right?"

Gordon's cheeks reddened, a welcome change from how pale he'd been. "I don't know what you're implying. I merely wanted to ask Astoria a question related to the theater."

"So how were you injured?" Hunter asked.

"As I said, I was going to Astoria's office." Gordon seemed to settle down and started speaking with more certainty. "But these corridors are dark, and I must have taken a wrong turn somewhere. It doesn't help that the rubbish in the hallways changes every time I walk back here."

"You walk the halls here often?" Jillian asked.

His cheeks pinked again, and he didn't meet her gaze. "I am interested in old architecture."

"So you found yourself lost," Hunter said, "but how did you

end up getting hurt?"

"I heard female voices ahead of me. I thought I'd finally found the right direction, so I picked up speed, which wasn't easy in this clutter. With all my scrambling, I made a lot of noise, and the voices stopped. Then I heard someone behind me. I thought it might be Astoria, so I spun around to see. I think I hit my head on something."

"You ran into something?" Jillian asked, her tone incredulous.

"I expect so," Gordon said. "I don't really remember, but there's so much stuff in the hallway. And it's dark."

"Could someone have hit you?" Jillian suggested.

"I believe I would have remembered that," Gordon insisted. "I have certainly never forgotten the last time someone clouted me on the head. No, I think I simply ran into something."

"But you're not sure," she said. "Maybe we should contact the sheriff. Or I could fetch Deputy Zane."

Gordon's blush darkened. "No, please, don't do that. This has all been very embarrassing."

"You should get medical attention, at the very least," Hunter said.

"I can drive you to the hospital," Jillian offered. "No one is really going to miss me at rehearsal."

"No." Gordon struggled to get to his feet. "I can't disappoint everyone. The show—or rather, the rehearsal must go on." He managed to stand up with a little help from Jillian, but he swayed unsteadily on his feet.

"Sorry, Gordon," Hunter said kindly, "but you're in no shape to rehearse. You need to see a doctor. It's best to check for concussions whenever you hit your head."

Gordon ran a hand over his face, which had gone pale again. "Maybe you're right. I do feel a bit dizzy."

"I'll take him, if you'll let me drive your car," Jillian said to Hunter. "That way, they're only down one major actor. I suppose

Melody could read Gordon's part for the rehearsal."

"Probably." Hunter pulled his keys from his pocket and handed them to Jillian. "But I'll help you get Gordon to the car."

"I'd appreciate that," Gordon said meekly.

The hallway was too tight for Jillian and Hunter to get on each side of Gordon, so Jillian mostly worked to clear the way as Hunter helped the injured man weave through the halls. They went out through the door to the theater lobby to avoid the delay that would surely come if everyone saw Gordon's injury.

As it was, a few people stood chatting in the lobby, and they rushed over as soon as Gordon shuffled through the door with Hunter supporting him on one side. Mrs. Winston led the charge, calling, "What happened?"

Gordon waved her off with his free hand. "Just a silly accident."

"Jillian is taking him to the hospital to be checked out," Hunter said. "But I'll be back in for rehearsal. Someone should tell Melody."

Two of the people turned and hurried into the auditorium.

Hunter insisted on helping Gordon all the way to the car. After Gordon was settled in the passenger seat, Jillian gave Hunter a quick hug. "You should get back to rehearsal. We'll be fine."

Hunter glanced at Gordon. "He doesn't seem to be nauseated and his pupils react to light—I saw that in the lobby. I think he should be fine to be driven instead of calling an ambulance."

Jillian wondered who Hunter was trying to convince, and she suspected it was himself. She knew his instincts to help were strong, and it was going to be hard for him to simply go inside. "They're counting on you in there too," she said gently. "And I can handle the driving." Then she gave him a saucy grin. "In fact, I'm really looking forward to it."

Hunter blinked at her in surprise. "Why?"

"Why would I want to drive your gorgeous Lexus?" She

tapped her chin. "How puzzling." She winked at him. "Go. I have to get moving."

On the drive to Nathan County Hospital, which lay almost exactly halfway between Moss Hollow and Painter's Ridge, Jillian listened to a flow of chatter from Gordon. It worked as a good barometer of his condition. He spoke clearly with no slurring. He also shared a considerable amount of information about Astoria Blaine.

"I doubt Astoria is going to be married much longer," Gordon said at one point. Jillian eyed him, and he flushed. "Not that it's any of my business."

Jillian repressed a chuckle. "The marriage isn't happy?"

"I don't know about that. How could a man not be happy to be married to someone as lovely as Astoria?"

Easily. "Then why would she stop being married?"

Gordon shifted in his seat, then winced and raised a hand to his head again, but he didn't remark on the headache he must have. "Her husband is quite ill. That's why he didn't come to the funeral. Astoria didn't actually say that the man's illness is fatal, not directly, but I could read between the lines."

"Don't you think it's a bit ghoulish to be waiting for the woman's poor husband to die?" Jillian asked.

"I don't know what you're talking about," Gordon said sulkily. "I was only making conversation." He folded his arms over his chest and fell silent.

Jillian asked him a few questions about his role in the play and he answered in snippy monosyllables. Fortunately, they were nearly to the hospital by that point, so she didn't experience the cold shoulder for long. Once they arrived, Gordon made a valiant effort to hop out and ignore Jillian, but his face went pale from the effort, and he didn't argue when she took his arm.

After checking in, they sat for a while in the emergency room's waiting area. Gordon was led out of the waiting room within the hour, and Jillian stayed behind. She walked a short way down the corridor and back for exercise, then settled down to pass the time by deleting unneeded photos from her phone.

"Jillian?"

Jillian raised her head and saw Lana Taylor, the nurse who was part of the maids' chorus. "Apparently I'm not the only one missing rehearsal tonight," Jillian said in greeting.

Lana smiled. "Duty called, and I had to fill in for another nurse who came down with the flu. I came out to let you know that the doctor is with Mr. Sprague. His tests look fine, and you should be able to take him home soon."

"Oh, that's good," Jillian said. "Now I just have to talk him out of going back to rehearsal."

Lana's expression darkened. "I'm not sure anyone needs to go back to rehearsal. There are too many injuries popping up at the theater. People were just starting to calm down after the last bout. With a new accident, I think they'll get worked up about it all over again."

"I hadn't heard anyone was worried about it."

Lana shrugged. "I think my uncle hears more about people's fears. A lot of folks take their anxiety to the doctor along with their aches." She gave Jillian a sly smile. "You know, I hear you're good at solving problems. Maybe you should take a crack at whatever's happening at the theater before someone else gets hauled in here."

"I don't know how much unraveling I can do. Astoria has banned me from the theater."

"Then how were you there to bring Gordon in?"

Jillian smiled sheepishly. "I don't always follow directions."

Lana laughed aloud. "And that's the kind of thinking that makes you good at solving mysteries." She reached out and tapped Jillian's arm lightly with the file folder she carried. "So keep thinking. If anyone can figure out what's going on, you can."

As Lana had predicted, Gordon walked out into the waiting area soon after, a bright white bandage standing out sharply on his bald pate. His pallor was much decreased, though he still seemed to be in poor spirits. "The doctor said I shouldn't be home alone," he said glumly. "I called my brother. I don't suppose you could drive me to his house? He's taking a cab to pick up my car from the theater and said he is definitely not driving all the way out here." Gordon grumbled about ungrateful siblings under his breath.

"I'll be happy to take you anywhere you need to go," Jillian said.

As they drove, Gordon shifted in his seat as if uncomfortable.

"Are you feeling all right?" Jillian asked.

"My head hurts a little," he said. "And I still feel guilty. The headache isn't that bad, and I'm not dizzy anymore. I should go back to rehearsal."

"You were at the hospital for a long time," Jillian said. "Rehearsal is probably over. And your brother is expecting you. You'll do a better job at the next rehearsal if you get some rest now."

"I suppose," Gordon said quietly.

"Also," Jillian added, "I thought your performance as the butler was impressive tonight. I don't know how much more rehearsal you need."

"I'm the murderer, you know."

Jillian turned to him in surprise for an instant, then realized he wasn't talking about Brittany but the play. *Obviously.* She was glad she hadn't embarrassed herself and said anything. She saw that Gordon was waiting for some kind of response, so she said, "It's an important part."

"I know, right? It's not considered a lead role, but this is a murder mystery, and I'm the killer. What role could be more important?"

The one who solves it? Jillian didn't comment, but she smiled over at him. The conversation seemed to mollify Gordon and he sat quietly for the rest of the ride.

Once Jillian dropped Gordon off at his brother's and had listened to the two men fuss at each other for a few minutes, she hopped back in Hunter's car and quickly texted him to ask if he was still at the theater. *Sorry to strand you*, she wrote.

No problem, he texted back. *Rehearsal still going.*

"Wow, that's commitment," she said aloud as she started the car. She headed for the theater, mildly fretting about her great-aunt and whether all this rehearsal time might be too much stress for Cornelia. Not to mention the fact that Jillian wasn't completely sure the theater was a safe place for any of them.

After she'd parked in the dark lot, Jillian trotted into the lobby—only to run into Astoria.

The tall, commanding woman clearly had not forgotten that she'd banned Jillian from the theater. "What are *you* doing here?"

"I'm here to pick up your male lead after driving Gordon Sprague, one of your actors, to the hospital," Jillian said.

Astoria's forehead furrowed ever so slightly. Jillian figured she was trying to work out whether Gordon was anyone important.

"He's a little bald man who thinks you're marvelous," Jillian added drily.

Astoria nodded. "Yes, I remember him. Is he going to be all right?"

"He's going to be fine, but I'm not convinced his injury was an accident. I'm not sure how many of the accidents here at the theater are truly accidents at all. Is there someone here who means to put a stop to the play?"

Jillian expected Astoria to reply to her question with hostility. Instead, the older woman paled so quickly that Jillian was actually afraid she might pass out.

"Whoa," Jillian said, reaching out for Astoria's arm. "Let's get you to a chair."

To her surprise, Astoria didn't resist. She let Jillian lead her to one of the chairs lined up against one wall.

"Do you know of someone who'd want to stop the play?" Jillian asked gently as soon as Astoria was seated.

Astoria shuddered. "I might," she said softly.

"Who?"

"My stepdaughter. Brittany."

Jillian sighed. "Brittany is dead, Mrs. Blaine."

"I'm not stupid." Astoria's voice sharpened to nearly her normal tone. "I know Brittany is dead."

"Then what are you talking about?"

Astoria swallowed hard. "Her ghost. I think the theater is haunted by my stepdaughter. And I think she's very angry."

"Angry at whom?" Jillian asked.

"At me. I think Brittany is after me. I think she wants me dead."

Jillian stared at the woman sitting in front of her. The thought briefly flittered through her head that she would almost not recognize Astoria Blaine as she was now, frightened and pale. "Why would Brittany want you dead?"

Astoria waved a long-fingered hand, gesturing vaguely around the lobby. "This place. It was Brittany's dream, or so she said. But it's financial deadweight, and I have to think about the good of the family."

"Which means?"

The pale woman thrust out her chin, a bit of her normal personality showing through. "I intend to sell it as soon as I line up a buyer. A theater is nothing but a hole to drop money into." As the words left Astoria's mouth, a chilly breeze seemed to pass through the lobby. Shivering, Jillian turned to see if the outside door was open, but the heavy double doors were closed and still.

Jillian's attention was jerked back to Astoria when the seated woman grabbed her arm in a clawlike grip. "Don't you see? I keep hearing her voice. And I know Brittany set that fire in my office. She tried to burn me to death."

"I thought that was faulty wiring," Jillian said.

Astoria's normal cold expression returned. "That's what they said, but I believe my stepdaughter caused it. She always hated me. She resented my marrying her father, and now she resents my need to sell this theater."

Jillian wondered briefly if Astoria was putting her on, but she didn't know how the woman could feign the sudden pallor. "I'm sure it's going to be all right."

"I'm not sure of anything of the sort," Astoria said, her tone still cold. "I'm afraid for Melody."

"Melody? I thought Brittany's ghost was angry with you."

Astoria narrowed her eyes at Jillian. "Don't mock me, young lady. I'm afraid for both of us and everyone here. Melody and Brittany were always competitive, even when they were little. But Brittany always won. Sometimes I truly believed Melody hated Brittany for always being the winner, including where their father was concerned. He made no secret that Brittany was his favorite. Now Melody has taken over Brittany's play. She's finally won. Brittany would hate that as much as she'd hate the sale of the theater."

Jillian folded her arms over her chest. "Maybe Brittany would be especially pleased with Melody for seeing her vision through. You're the only one trying to put an end to it."

"I'm not ending the play," Astoria insisted. "I want the show to open. We need the ticket sales, and a successful show will make the theater worth more."

"Where are you when you hear Brittany's voice?" Jillian didn't believe in ghosts, but she wondered if someone might be intentionally terrorizing Astoria. The woman certainly knew how to rub people the wrong way. In fact, the only person she'd heard speak well of the woman was Gordon.

"My office, mostly," Astoria said. "Sometimes the backstage corridors. But Melody heard her too, once, when she was on the stage. She didn't say anything about it, but I'm sure she heard."

"What does Brittany's ghost say?"

"I can't tell. She sounds angry, but the words aren't clear." Astoria raised a shaking hand to her temple. "It's terrifying."

Jillian could think of two people connected to the play who were clearly unhappy. Helene had thought Brittany wanted to get rid of her, but Jillian couldn't imagine why Helene might pretend to be Brittany. Porter, on the other hand, seemed to be a ticking time bomb, and she could easily see him directing his anger at Astoria and Melody. But could the man copy Brittany's voice?

And what Astoria had said about Melody gave Jillian pause as well. If Melody and Brittany had been in competition their whole lives, could the younger sister have done something to ensure that she finally won? If she had—or even if Porter simply suspected she had—that might inspire him to torment Melody.

Astoria's sly tone cut into Jillian's thoughts. "You're welcome to be in the play and come to the theater," she said, "if you'll do me a favor."

"We're not making free desserts for you," Jillian said quickly.

"That wasn't what I had in mind, though you *should*." Astoria folded her hands in her lap almost demurely and lowered her head, peering at Jillian through her fringe of expertly applied false eyelashes. "I never should have buried Brittany here, so close to the theater where she died, but I thought it was best to have the whole funeral business done quickly. And now she's haunting me."

"So what's the favor?"

"I need help putting Brittany's spirit to rest. This is the South. Surely you can find me some witchy person."

"Witchy person?" Jillian echoed, raising both eyebrows.

"Yes, someone who deals in these things. Everyone knows Southerners are all superstitious, so you probably have half a dozen backwoods friends who talk to ghosts."

Surprise wrestled with offense inside Jillian as she tried to think of a comeback. Sure, she knew someone who believed in ghosts and thought she could chat with them, but she was hardly going to suggest Cornelia to this horrible woman. Instead, she gave Astoria a withering gaze. "Well, I know one person who clearly believes in ghosts, but I understand she's from New York."

Astoria opened her mouth, clearly ready to say, "Who?"

Then she must have realized Jillian's implication, and her mouth snapped shut. They stared silently at one another for a moment before Astoria finally said, "Does that mean you won't help me?"

"I *might* be willing to help you figure out who is pretending to be a ghost. For the safety of everyone else involved in this production."

Before Astoria could respond to that, the doors from the theater to the lobby swung open. Rehearsal was over. In a flash, Jillian was surrounded by people asking questions about Gordon.

"Gordon is fine," she assured the crowd. She took a few steps away from Astoria so she could watch the doors for Hunter. "The hospital released him, and he's spending the night with his brother."

Relief was clear on every face, and one of the older men made a joke about Gordon's having a hard head that brought more laughter than it warranted. Jillian turned toward Astoria, intending to make a snide comment about how nice it was that *everyone* was concerned about one of her actors, but the chair was empty. The older woman was gone.

Cornelia came out with Hunter beside her. "Oh, how is Gordon?" Cornelia asked.

Jillian repeated her update on Gordon's condition, and Hunter added, "See? I told you Jillian had texted me about it."

Cornelia harrumphed. "Texting will never replace talking."

Not in Moss Hollow, anyway, Jillian thought wryly. But all she said was, "Do you need a ride home?"

Cornelia shook her head. "I'm waiting on Lucille and Vera. We're going to grab a cup of decaf and decompress." Jillian recognized the names. Lucille and Vera were two of the women from the gardening club.

"I'll see you at home later," Jillian said, giving her great-aunt a quick hug.

Cornelia beamed at her and patted her cheek. "You're a good

egg for taking Gordon to the hospital. I'm relieved to hear he's all right." She looked past Jillian's shoulder. "There's Lucille and Vera now. Good night, darlings."

"Darlings?" Hunter echoed after Cornelia had hurried off.

"Aunt Cornelia has gone a little Hollywood, I think," Jillian said. "I have to admit, I'll be glad when this play business is over. It's made everyone a little loopy."

"Present company excluded, I hope," Hunter said.

Jillian laughed and slipped her arm through his. "You, Hunter Greyson, are the least loopy person I have ever met."

Much of the lobby had cleared while they had been chatting with Cornelia, so they strolled outside, in no particular hurry. The moon had emerged from behind the clouds, and Jillian noticed for the first time that it was full. "A full moon should help brighten up the parking area a little," she said. "Though they definitely need actual lights installed."

"There are a few mounted on the walls of the building," Hunter said. "They simply aren't on."

Jillian huffed. "Probably a cost-saving choice. Astoria was complaining about the theater expenses earlier."

Hunter paused, pulling Jillian to a stop. "You saw Astoria?"

Jillian nodded. "I was talking to her in the lobby, but she disappeared when the rehearsal let out."

"And she didn't try to call the sheriff to report your defying her banishment?" Hunter asked, his voice still surprised.

"She started out that way, but it turns out she wants something from me."

"Free pastries?"

Jillian shook her head. "Not this time. She thinks she's being haunted and is searching for an exorcist."

"Astoria Blaine believes in ghosts?"

"She seems to believe in this one. She told me Brittany is

haunting the theater, and she claimed to have heard Brittany's voice."

Hunter's brows drew together. "Do you believe her?"

"I believe she's experienced something. She was deathly pale and shaking when she told me about it. She said she believes Brittany tried to kill her with the fire in her office."

"I thought that was faulty wiring."

"So I was told. I'm a little concerned that Astoria is losing it. Sometimes tightly wound people can be pushed over the edge." Jillian scanned the area around the dark sidewalk. The bustle of other actors had cleared, and they were alone. "Astoria clearly had a bad relationship with Brittany. She said her stepdaughter hated her."

"Those relationships can be difficult, but I don't believe in ghosts."

"Neither do I," Jillian said, "but I do believe someone might be playing ghost."

"I don't know. Guilt can weigh heavily on a person. It's possible Astoria is imagining things."

"Does she really seem to be a woman who imagines things?" Jillian asked.

"Not so much, but we never really know what goes on inside someone else's head."

Jillian didn't argue with that. Instead, she asked, "What do you think of Melody? Do you still like her?"

"Sure. She's putting her all into the play. And I'll admit to preferring her style of direction. I haven't had to peel her off of me a single time."

"I appreciate that myself," Jillian said. "Astoria said Melody and Brittany competed a lot."

Hunter winced. "That couldn't have gone well for Melody."

"According to Astoria, it didn't. This is Melody's first real win over her sister, taking over the play. Astoria thinks it's why

Brittany is haunting Melody too. Apparently, she has also heard her sister's voice."

"That's interesting. It might be worth asking Melody about it. Are you going to tell all of this to Laura Lee?"

"If you think I should." Jillian thought for a moment. "I ought to call her anyway. I want to know exactly when Melody arrived in Moss Hollow." As Jillian said that, she spotted movement from the corner of her eye, near the shadow thrown by the corner of the building. She tensed and whipped her head in that direction.

"What's the matter?" Hunter asked, his gaze following hers.

"I saw someone over there." Jillian pointed.

"I'm sure we're not the only ones who loitered a bit before heading for our car."

Jillian was unconvinced. "But we didn't loiter in the shadows. I think someone was spying on us."

Seeming to notice how concerned she was, Hunter took her hand. "Maybe it was just someone who wanted to hear your theories about Brittany's murder without revealing their presence. In any case, let's get going." He tugged her toward his car.

Jillian didn't say anything else, but she glanced back into the darkness more than once, wondering who overheard her suspicions about Melody—and worrying what that person might do as a result.

Although Jillian had to work the front counter at the bakery the next day while Maggie stepped out to run an errand, she was pleased to no longer be on the receiving end of skeptical glances from the customers. Everybody chattered about the upcoming play, but no one looked askance at Jillian anymore. *Apparently, my days as a murder suspect are over.*

At one point, Gordon Sprague walked in, the bandage on his forehead bright white under the lights. He was practically mobbed by the rest of the customers, all voicing their relief that he was all right or their sympathy for his bump on the head. It was clear that Gordon enjoyed every moment of the attention.

"What can I get you, Gordon?" Jillian asked.

"I'll take two cream puffs, please," he answered, then dropped his voice. "Melody told me they're her mother's favorite."

"That's generous of you," Jillian said, trying for a noncommittal tone. She still thought Gordon's behavior was inappropriate considering Astoria was a married woman, but since she was fairly sure it was never going to go beyond free cream puffs, she decided to keep her thoughts to herself.

"She works such long hours on behalf of the play, which is a gift to all of Moss Hollow," Gordon explained. "It's only fair that we return the favor."

Jillian settled the cream puffs in a white box lined with parchment paper. "Sure." Her tone must not have been as neutral as she hoped, because his cheeks flushed and he was a little sulky for the rest of the transaction. She took his money and thanked him cheerily.

After Gordon left, the chatter about the play increased still more. Not many of the customers had actually met Astoria Blaine, but they all seemed to have opinions. Jillian did her best to let it remain background noise as she filled boxes and bags with pastries—but it was a losing battle, and soon all she could think about was Astoria.

By the time Maggie got back from her errand, Jillian was seriously ready to escape into the back. She walked right through the kitchen and ducked into the storeroom to call Laura Lee.

The deputy answered right away. "Hi, Jillian. I didn't see you last night after you found Gordon. I heard he's all right."

"I saw him a little while ago. He was in the bakery buying pastries for Astoria, so he's fine."

"Why would he buy pastries for that woman?" Laura Lee asked, her voice incredulous. "I do believe Astoria Blaine would turn everyone in Moss Hollow into her free help if given half a chance."

"Ah, so you've chatted with the lady."

"I'm not sure I'd use that word to describe her." Laura Lee sighed. "Don't listen to me. I'm in a rotten mood. We all are. No one wants to have a murder here go unsolved, and we're not seeing any real movement on the case."

"I actually have a question related to it and a little story to tell. Which do you want first?"

"The story, please," Laura Lee said. "I always enjoy hearing about the tidbits that fall into your lap."

Jillian leaned against one of the strong, built-in shelving units in the storeroom and told Laura Lee about her conversation with Astoria, beginning with her banishment from the play and ending with Astoria's request for a ghost handler. When she finished, the deputy was silent on the other end of the phone. Jillian waited, then prompted her friend. "Laura Lee, you still there?"

"Yeah, hold on. I'm taking notes, and you talk fast."

"No one in the South talks fast," Jillian said, stretching her light Southern accent into a molasses-thick drawl.

"It must have been all your years in California. Unhealthy. So, do you think she really believes the theater is haunted?"

"I don't know. It doesn't seem consistent with her personality, but she went pale as paper while telling me about hearing Brittany's voice."

"Are you going to send Cornelia over to commune with the ghost?" Laura Lee asked.

"Absolutely not. In fact, I'd ask her to drop out of the play if I stood any chance of convincing her. I don't like the 'accident' rate with this play, and Brittany's unsolved murder isn't sitting well with me either."

"Thanks," Laura Lee said drily. "We're doing our best."

"I know you are. I didn't mean that as criticism. I'm just worried."

"I know the feeling. Say, you mentioned having a question for me. What's that?"

"I was wondering, when did Melody arrive in Moss Hollow? Was Brittany still alive when her sister got here?"

"You suspect Melody?" Laura Lee sounded skeptical. "She doesn't really seem likely. I actually saw tears in her eyes at one point during the funeral."

"Her stepmother said she competed with Brittany for years and always lost," Jillian said. "There had to be a lot of frustration from that."

"I suppose. We did check, of course. Both Melody and Astoria reported arriving after Brittany's death, though they didn't travel together. Astoria was in New York City dealing with some family business prior to coming here. Her secretary vouched for her. And Melody left from the family estate, as confirmed by a maid."

"So their alibis were both people in their employ. People who easily might lie for them."

"At the time, we weren't really scrutinizing either of them. I thought you favored the stage manager as the killer, or the choreographer."

"I'm not marking anyone off my list," Jillian said. "I'm enlarging it. What alibis did Porter and Helene have, by the way?"

"None really," Laura Lee answered. "Helene said she was at the inn. She's staying at the Southern Peach Inn, though no one saw her that day."

"The Southern Peach?" Jillian whistled. "She must have some money. A long-term stay there cannot be cheap."

"Definitely not. The stage manager is staying at the theater as a kind of caretaker. There's a little apartment attached. At any rate, no one saw him, and he was on the property at the time of the murder."

"Oh," Jillian said softly. "That's interesting."

"He's an odd bird too. We're watching him."

Jillian's mind whirred with the new information from Laura Lee. "Thanks for updating me. And since I'm back in the play, I guess I'll see you at rehearsals."

After she hung up, Jillian felt a desperate urge for a cup of coffee and headed back to the front. As she was pouring, the door to the bakery opened. Jillian glanced up, and to her surprise, she saw Melody Blaine join the line at the counter.

Jillian sipped from her mug and watched Melody through her lashes. The young woman appeared almost buoyantly happy. Though Melody had generally been pleasant before, Jillian saw her call out to one of the seated customers in a friendly way and say kind things about the woman's singing in the musical. As Jillian watched Melody, she almost felt guilty about suspecting her in Brittany's murder.

When Melody reached the counter, Jillian stepped up to wait on her, getting a surprised glance from Maggie when she edged in front of her. Fortunately, Maggie didn't ask questions, instead edging aside to putter around straightening displays.

"You seem to be having a good day," Jillian said to Melody.

"I'm having a fantastic day," Melody enthused. "My dad has been sick, really sick. The doctors couldn't figure out what was wrong, either. Honestly, I've been worried half to death, but today I talked to his nurse and he's doing much, much better."

"I'm so glad to hear that." Jillian offered a smile. "What can I get you?"

"Coffee and a cheese Danish, please."

"For here or to go?" Jillian asked. Melody seemed to think about that for a moment, so Jillian added, "If you have time, maybe we could sit down together? I'm really supposed to be on a break myself." Jillian heard Maggie snort, but she managed to make it sound like a sneeze.

"That's so nice," Melody said. "I'd enjoy that, though I can't chat long. My to-do list is crazy."

"Mine too," Jillian said as she wrapped a Danish in parchment and handed it to Melody. A coffee appeared on the counter almost magically, and Jillian caught Maggie's knowing grin before the young woman ducked back out of the way again.

Once they were seated at one of the empty tables, Jillian said, "The play seems to be going smoothly. You're doing a great job as director. You bring out the best in everyone."

The young woman beamed, and Jillian wondered how often Melody had gotten positive feedback in her life. "Everyone is working so hard," Melody said. "That makes all the difference."

"The town is very enthusiastic about the play," Jillian agreed.

Melody took a long sip of her coffee, then sighed. "It's wonderful. I do believe I could live here forever and do play after play."

"It doesn't sound as if that's going to happen," Jillian said, feeling a guilty pang as Melody's face fell. "Astoria said she's going to sell the theater."

"I know." The effort Melody put into smiling was almost painful. "But if the buyer keeps the building as a theater, they'll need a director. And if this play is really good, that could be me. At least, I hope so."

Jillian took a sip of her own coffee, using it to think. "Why not ask your stepmother to let you keep the theater? Brittany had clearly intended to keep it."

"I know, but Brittany was always so—" Melody paused, nibbling on her lower lip as she chose her next words. "Forceful. Headstrong. Plus, our father wouldn't hear of disappointing Brittany. But now with my stepmother in charge . . ." She sighed again. "No one talks Astoria into anything. Father is the only one who has ever been able to rein her in, really, and he's been so sick lately."

"He's doing better though," Jillian encouraged.

Melody brightened again. "Yes, he is." She leaned over and whispered, "I'm hoping he feels well enough to come down for the play's opening night. I'd love for him to see it."

"I hope he does," Jillian said, and found she truly meant it.

Melody chattered on for a bit about some last-minute wardrobe changes for the play, and then she switched to fretting about whether she should keep the trapdoor exit by the villain in one of the last scenes. "It's dramatic, but every time we rehearse it, I worry about that trapdoor."

"You don't think it's safe?"

"I don't know, but it also seems kind of disrespectful. I mean, my sister's body was found there."

"Are you worried about your sister haunting you?"

Melody sat back, blinking at Jillian. "What a silly thing to say." Then she put a hand over her mouth. "I'm sorry. That was rude. Do you believe in ghosts?"

"No, but your stepmother believes Brittany is haunting

the theater."

Melody laughed merrily, then noticed Jillian wasn't laughing along. "You're not kidding."

"No," Jillian said. "You didn't know?"

"My stepmother doesn't believe in ghosts. Astoria is probably the least fanciful person you'll ever meet. One of the first things she did after she married Father was announce to Brittany and me that there was no Santa Claus, and the family wasn't going to indulge in silliness like that." Melody rolled her eyes. "I was *five*!"

"She told me last night that she's been hearing Brittany's voice in the theater and that she believes it's a ghost. She said you've heard it too."

"I think my stepmother must be making fun of you somehow," Melody said. "I haven't heard any voices. I mean, I do sometimes enjoy thinking about ghosts. The idea is so romantic, especially since the theater is in such an old building. But I'm sure my sister's spirit isn't moping around the theater." Then she smiled a little. "Though if anyone were going to come back from the dead and complain, it would be Brittany."

"So this is the first you've heard about a ghost?" Jillian asked.

Melody nodded, then a rueful smile touched her mouth. "You know, this would explain why Porter has stayed on, considering he shows every sign of hating my stepmother's guts—I wasn't kidding when I thought it was possible he tried to kill her, you know. And he's not overly fond of me either. Maybe he believes Brittany is still around."

"What makes you think he hates Astoria, or you?"

"He's not exactly subtle with the scowling and mumbling," Melody said. "Honestly, I'm surprised Astoria doesn't fire him, even with how little he charges. Still, I'm really glad we don't have sandbags hanging from the rafters like in old theater mysteries. I'd worry about one dropping on my head."

For some reason, Jillian felt a chill. "Porter was very fond of your sister. Did she feel the same about him?"

"'Fond' is not the word for how he feels," Melody said. "'Obsessed' fits better. Brittany used to call him 'that super creep,' but he's one of the best stage managers in the business, or so Brittany said. Anyway, she used his obvious fixation to get him to work really cheap. And I have to admit, it's probably worth putting up with the weirdness. The man can fix anything. He's practically a mechanical genius."

"I wonder if he ever figured out that she was taking advantage of him," Jillian said.

"He doesn't act it. He still criticizes whenever I make any changes from what Brittany wanted." Melody set her cup on the table. "I must sound awful. Brittany and I really didn't get along most of the time. Well, pretty much all of the time. But now I sort of miss her. Isn't that weird?"

"Family is weird," Jillian said gently.

Melody picked up her cup again. "I'll drink to that." She drained the last of the coffee, then stood. "And on that note, I really have to run. I have a million errands. It was nice to talk to you."

"I enjoyed it too," Jillian said, getting a sweet smile from the young woman before she left the bakery.

Jillian bussed the table, then walked back to the kitchen in time to get a scolding from Bertie about the number of orders they had to fill. Impulsively, Jillian hugged her grandmother, jostling the clipboard full of orders in her hand.

When Jillian let go, Bertie flushed and waved the clipboard at Jillian. "Enough of that nonsense. Get to work."

But Jillian wasn't fooled. She could see that Bertie was pleased.

To make up for her dillydallying, Jillian focused on filling orders for the rest of the morning and took her lunch break in the bakery kitchen, eating a sandwich she'd brought from home. As a result, they had finished the last of the orders when Cornelia swept in late in the afternoon.

"Jillian," Cornelia scolded, wiggling a finger at her. "Shame on you for not telling me about Astoria Blaine's great need."

Oh no.

Bertie glanced up from the worktable she was scrubbing. "If that woman has tried to rope you into providing free food for her silly meeting, you need to go back and tell her no."

"Free food?" Cornelia echoed. "Not at all. I'm talking about lending spiritual assistance."

"Isn't that Pastor Keith's area of expertise?" Bertie asked.

Cornelia stamped a foot as if her sister were being intentionally obtuse. "I'm talking about making contact with the ghost in the theater."

"There's no ghost in the theater," Jillian said, unable to keep exhaustion out of her voice.

"There is, and you knew about it," Cornelia scolded. "Luckily, I had called the theater to talk to Melody about the possibility of expanding my role the tiniest bit. I could help take some of the strain off poor Gordon since his accident."

"Shame on you for taking advantage of Gordon's injury!" Bertie exclaimed.

Cornelia ignored her twin, keeping her attention on Jillian. "Fortunately, Astoria answered, and apparently she'd heard about my affinity for the spirit realm."

Because Moss Hollow is full of gossips. Jillian didn't share her feelings, but she suspected it was all over her face since her great-aunt frowned in her direction.

"She asked me to come and cleanse the theater of the ghost of Brittany Blaine. She's worried that her stepdaughter means her harm."

"You need to stay out of it," Bertie insisted.

Cornelia thrust out her chin. "You are not the boss of me, Bertie Harper."

"Fine." Bertie slammed her hands down on the table, then pointed at Jillian. "In that case, you go with her and make sure she stays out of trouble."

Sure. Since that's always so easy.

Cornelia insisted upon taking her beloved Mustang, but she cheerfully let Jillian drive. Once they got to the theater, Jillian offered to carry the quilted tote bag her great-aunt had brought. She should have been suspicious at the eager way Cornelia handed it over, but the weight still surprised her. "What do you have in here?"

"All the things I may need to connect with Brittany's haint," Cornelia said.

"Like what? Bricks?"

Cornelia didn't answer. She merely squared her shoulders and marched toward the theater as if going into battle.

Jillian watched her for a moment, fighting the urge to chuckle at Cornelia's ramrod-straight posture. *Well, she is going to have to deal with Astoria. That might be worth a little shoulder squaring.*

To Jillian's surprise, Astoria was waiting for them in the lobby, sitting in the same chair she'd taken after the rehearsal. When they entered, the tall woman stood and strode toward them on dangerously high heels.

"Thank you for coming," she said to Cornelia, then gave Jillian a reproving glare. "You could have told me your aunt might be able to help with my problem."

"I would have," Jillian said, "if she could."

Both Astoria and Cornelia gave her matching narrow-eyed glares.

Cornelia smiled at Astoria. "I cannot guarantee that I'll be able to make contact with Brittany, of course. But from what you described, it sounds as though your daughter is eager to communicate."

"*Step*daughter," Astoria corrected. "Where do you want to begin?"

"You said you mostly hear the sounds in your office," Jillian suggested, thinking that she might get something out of the visit after all if she had the chance to poke around in Astoria's office.

"That's true," Astoria said, though she kept her eyes on Cornelia. "Do you think that's best?"

To Jillian's disappointment, Cornelia said, "I think we should begin on the stage. Ghosts in theaters are drawn to the stage. That's a well-documented phenomenon. In fact, many theaters have the tradition of keeping a ghost light burning on the stage at all times for the sake of spectral performers." She leaned slightly toward Astoria. "Do you have a ghost light?"

"I am sure we don't," Astoria said. "It sounds like it would raise the electric bill, which is already quite high enough."

"I see. Well, you might want to think about getting one."

Before Astoria could comment, Cornelia turned and swept dramatically through the doors leading to the auditorium. Jillian hefted the heavy tote bag up onto her shoulder and followed along in her great-aunt's wake.

After an exasperated huff, Astoria came along as well. "I want you to convince Brittany to move on," she commanded, though Cornelia didn't respond. "It is extremely important that opening night go off without a hitch."

Jillian glanced over her shoulder. "Why is that?"

"There will be a number of potential buyers in the audience," Astoria said, her tone full of annoyance. "It seems no one is willing to commit to making an offer until they see the theater at work. So, a successful opening night is imperative, and I do not see how a haunting would be a positive addition. I want the buyers to be impressed, not horrified."

"I don't know," Jillian said. "Some theaters seem to go to great lengths to publicize their ghosts. It's a kind of tourist attraction."

Astoria huffed. "That is not the kind of venue I am attempting to sell."

"I will do my best to convince Brittany," Cornelia said loftily. "But it is very difficult to force spirits into specific behaviors."

"Fine, fine," Astoria said. "Just do what you can. Remember, this is good for Moss Hollow."

"Does that mean you're not going to pay my aunt for her time?" Jillian asked. Though she wasn't certain Cornelia was going to do anything worthy of pay, she still hated the idea of her family doing free labor for this imperious woman.

"Your aunt volunteered," Astoria said. "For the good of the community. I was pleased to see *someone* in your family has community spirit."

Jillian didn't bother rising to the bait since they'd reached the stage. She walked close to Cornelia as the older woman climbed the steps. The drawing room set was still in place, including a settee and a small table with two chairs. Cornelia settled into one of the chairs and held out her hands for her bag. Jillian set it on the table with a huff of breath, glad to have the weight off her shoulder.

Cornelia reached into the bag and pulled out a large scented candle, the kind that came in a heavy glass jar with a lid. Then she pulled out a second just like it.

Well, that explains the weight.

Cornelia set the candles on the table and pulled off the lids. "These candles will serve the purpose of a ghost light to draw Brittany's spirit."

"Just do whatever you have to," Astoria said, looking down her long nose at Cornelia. "I put up with that girl enough when she was alive. I don't want her here now."

Cornelia gave Astoria a quelling glance. "Please, clear your mind of negative emotions. Breathe deeply and slowly."

Jillian took a deep breath, figuring she might as well go along with Cornelia's show. The scent of cinnamon filled the air, no doubt coming from the candles. It intensified after Cornelia lit them. Then, Jillian's great-aunt reached into the bag and pulled out a small bundle wrapped in a brightly patterned silk scarf. She placed the bundle on the table near the candles. "I read that silk helps charge the cards," she whispered to Jillian.

Cornelia carefully unfolded the scarf, revealing her stack of subscription cards torn from magazines. Jillian heard Astoria's restless movement beside her and looked up to see the tall woman frowning as Cornelia carefully shuffled the subscription cards.

"What are those for?" Astoria asked.

"The tear-out cards will allow me to communicate with Brittany," Cornelia said, her voice high and eerie. Jillian suspected she was imitating some of the psychics from old movies. "I use them often to communicate with the Belle Haven haint."

Astoria's eyebrows shot up. "Haint?"

"Ghost," Jillian answered. "It's an old legend."

"And your aunt speaks with her using trash?"

Jillian shrugged. *If you're expecting me to explain Cornelia, I can't help you.* "You asked her to come," was all she whispered back.

"Quiet, please!" Cornelia commanded.

For an instant, Jillian thought Astoria was going to snap at her, but the scowling woman merely nodded and crossed her arms over her chest, glaring down at Cornelia as she fiddled with her tear-out cards.

"Brittany!" Cornelia called out in her theatrical, breathy tone. "Speak to us."

To everyone's shock, they immediately heard a voice that Jillian recognized as Brittany's irritable tone. However, try as she might, Jillian couldn't make out the words.

"Why can't we understand her?" Astoria asked in a desperate tone.

Jillian glanced at the woman and saw that she had gone pale again. Astoria no longer stood with her arms crossed defiantly. Instead, she seemed to hug herself protectively against the sound.

Cornelia also seemed more than a little overwhelmed. Jillian was certain her great-aunt had never had so much "success" with her efforts to contact the Belle Haven haint. Finally, she took a deep breath and called, "Brittany, what would you say to your mother?"

"*Step*mother!" Astoria hissed.

The voice continued to mutter and scold, but it didn't become any clearer. Cornelia turned her attention to the pile of paper scraps, flipping several over. One was a subscription card from a mystery magazine with the word *murder* emblazoned on it. "You want to talk about your murder?" Cornelia asked. "Do you want to tell us who your murderer is?"

"Just tell her to leave!" Astoria commanded.

"Spirits often refuse to leave until their conflicts are resolved." Cornelia flipped another card. This was one she'd collected from a hairdressing magazine at the Clip & Curl.

"Those are useless magazine subscription cards," Astoria said. "They can't tell you anything."

Jillian almost smiled. *That's the first sensible thing I've heard since we got here.*

"They can if Brittany chooses," Cornelia said breathily. "Speak, Brittany. Speak."

At Cornelia's call, the sound of Brittany's voice suddenly stopped. Jillian held her breath, waiting for the voice to begin again, but the theater remained eerily quiet.

"Brittany," Cornelia called out, making Jillian jump. "What do you want to say to your stepmother?" She revealed another subscription card. This one must have come from Greyson

& Sons, as it was from a funeral director's trade magazine. It showed a casket.

"I knew it. She wants me dead!" Astoria shrieked, then she clutched her chest and fell to the floor.

At that exact moment, a shot rang out.

Jillian instantly made the connection with Brittany's stunt on the first day of auditions, but this definitely wasn't a blank. The bullet struck a vase on a plinth directly behind where Astoria had been standing, causing an explosion of glass.

18

Jillian pulled Cornelia out of her chair and to the floor behind the table. Though no other shots rang out, they huddled under the table as Jillian pulled out her phone and called for help, quickly describing the shooting and reporting that one woman was unconscious but not shot.

Neither Jillian nor Cornelia spoke again, merely clutching each other as they crouched on the stage. Jillian shifted position as silently as possible when her calves began to ache, and she noticed then that Astoria was beginning to move. Frightened that the shooter might try again if the older woman sat up, Jillian leaned toward Astoria and whispered, "Don't move. The shooter may still be here."

Astoria turned terrified eyes toward her, but she didn't say anything, and she didn't try to get up.

The response from the sheriff's department was quick, though it certainly didn't feel that way. Deputies poured in through the double doors at the back of the auditorium. Jillian saw Gooder, Laura Lee, and Tom split up as soon as they entered so each could head for the stage down a different aisle. Sheriff Coy Henderson came through the doors next and followed Gooder down the center aisle.

"Everyone all right?" Sheriff Henderson called out.

"I think so," Jillian said. "Mrs. Blaine may need medical attention, but no one has been hit."

"I do not need medical attention," Astoria insisted haughtily.

When he reached the stage, Gooder asked, "Which direction did the shots come from?"

Jillian pointed toward the backstage wing. "Judging from how the shot hit the vase, I think the person must have been back there."

He nodded without answering and headed toward the wings. Sheriff Henderson knelt next to Astoria, shielding her with his body as he helped her up. "Can you walk?" he asked. "I can carry you if you can't."

"Of course I can walk," Astoria said, much to Jillian's relief. Though Astoria was thin, Jillian doubted carrying grown women around would be good for Sheriff Henderson's heart.

The sheriff waved for Jillian and Cornelia to join him. "Let's get you ladies out of here."

"I'm all for that," Cornelia said as Jillian helped her up.

When Jillian saw Cornelia limping a little, she whispered, "Are you all right?"

"A little stiff is all," her great-aunt answered. "I don't spend a lot of time sitting on hard floors."

Jillian and Cornelia led the way off the stage and down the aisle. With every step, Jillian flinched in anticipation of another gunshot, but the theater was quiet except for the sound of the deputies rustling around as they searched. They exited into the lobby in time to meet the paramedics coming through the front doors.

The sheriff ordered Astoria into a chair, where the medics began checking her vitals, much to her clear embarrassment.

The sheriff led Jillian and Cornelia a short distance away. "Tell me exactly what happened."

"We were on the stage," Jillian said. "And we were having a stressful interaction. Astoria clutched her chest and crumpled at the same moment that a shot rang out. I might have thought it was a blank—a gun was fired in here before with a blank in it—but a vase shattered, and I knew it had been hit. Cornelia and I hid behind a table, and I called for help."

The sheriff immediately locked on the one vague sentence. "Why was it a stressful interaction?"

"Because of the ghost," Cornelia said, and Jillian winced. She'd been hoping to avoid discussing the "ghost," or at least Cornelia's efforts to contact it, but she should have realized the futility of that. She didn't feel better when Cornelia added, "Though I'm almost certain the ghost did not shoot at us."

"Ghost?" The lines in the sheriff's face deepened in confusion. "Is that a character in the play?"

"No, *Brittany's* ghost," Cornelia said. Jillian considered grabbing her great-aunt and dragging her away, but she suspected the sheriff would stop her. "She has manifested in the theater several times, so Astoria asked me to come and try to put Brittany to rest, which I was more than happy to do. The manifestation was fascinating, and everything was going well. I believe we were making real headway in communicating with Brittany until someone shot at us."

The sheriff took a long look at her. "Sometimes it's hard to believe you're Bertie Harper's twin sister."

Cornelia nodded. "I know. Bertie is so closed off to the spirit realm. It's sad really, and I think it's frustrating for the Belle Haven haint."

The sheriff turned to Jillian. "And you were part of this ghost thing?"

Jillian held up her hands. "I drove Cornelia over. Bertie insisted she not come on her own."

He snuck a glance back at Cornelia. "I can see why."

Cornelia poked Jillian. "Tell him about the manifestation. He seems to believe you more than me."

Sheriff Henderson narrowed his eyes. "What manifestation?"

"We did hear a voice, and it certainly sounded like Brittany," Jillian said. "But I couldn't tell you where the voice came from or what it said. It was muffled."

"Spirits have great difficulty crossing the veil," Cornelia said helpfully.

The sheriff winced, but he kept his eyes on Jillian.

Jillian continued, "I would have guessed that someone is playing a mean joke on Mrs. Blaine—up until the gunshot. There was nothing funny about that. If she hadn't collapsed right before the shot, the bullet could easily have hit her."

"How certain are you that the voice belonged to the deceased?" the sheriff asked.

"I didn't really know Brittany Blaine, but I had heard her talk on more than one occasion. It sounded like her to me. And Mrs. Blaine identified it as Brittany's voice." Jillian thought again about the sound of Brittany's voice versus her sister's. The difference was mostly intonation. She'd never heard Melody speak in that kind of harsh, hateful tone. But that didn't mean she *couldn't*.

"Something else?" the sheriff prompted.

Jillian considered telling him her thoughts, but it was only conjecture. "I don't know if it was a recording of some kind or someone imitating Brittany's voice."

"Or a ghost," Cornelia interjected.

"I'm pretty sure it wasn't that," Jillian said.

Cornelia shook her head dolefully. "She's exactly like my sister sometimes."

"I do wonder . . ." Jillian's voice trailed off. She wasn't entirely sure if commenting was the right thing to do.

"Wonder what?" the sheriff asked, an edge coming into his voice. The ghost stuff was clearly beginning to irritate him. Sheriff Coy Henderson had never been one to suffer fools or foolish ideas.

"I wonder where Melody was during the shooting. She has some performing experience, I believe. It's possible she could imitate Brittany's voice well enough, especially since it was muffled. Mrs. Blaine intends to sell the theater, but Melody wants to keep it."

"That's worth looking into, I suppose," the sheriff said.

The doors to the theater opened, and Gooder walked out holding a plastic bag with a handgun in it. "I found this laying on the floor in the wings. It's loaded with live rounds, and it has definitely been fired."

"There's a gun used in the play," Jillian said. "That might be it."

"They use a real gun in the play?" the sheriff asked.

"Yes," Cornelia said. "But only to fire a blank offstage to signify the murder in the story. The play is a murder mystery. *Murderous Intentions.*"

"Swell," the sheriff said drily.

"The ammunition in this weapon is real now," Gooder said.

The sheriff pointed at the gun. "Secure that and rejoin the search. I want to talk to anyone you find in the theater." He returned his attention to Jillian and Cornelia. "We'll check the gun for prints. Hopefully the shooter used it without gloves. I'd say we need prints from you two for exclusionary purposes, but I'm pretty sure we have you on file."

"You do," Jillian said drily. "I've been excluded a lot."

"Me too," Cornelia added.

"Good," the sheriff said. "You two can go. But be careful. It seems someone is intent on a second murder. And for some reason, anytime someone in this town decides to kill someone, they seem happy to add you to the list, Miss Green. As much of an intrusion as you are on my investigations sometimes, I'd rather that didn't happen."

"Thank you, Sheriff," Jillian said, and then she hustled Cornelia out of the theater.

As they headed to the parking lot, Jillian remembered again the car that nearly ran her over and slowed her pace, checking her surroundings carefully. She only saw Cornelia's Mustang, several sheriff's department vehicles, and a flashy, expensive car with New

York plates that likely belonged to Astoria. Jillian paused in front of it. Astoria must have driven down from New York, not flown. That would make it harder to know exactly when she'd arrived. She wondered if Melody had driven as well.

"What?" Cornelia asked, tugging on Jillian's arm. "You've got your sleuthing face on."

Jillian rolled her eyes. "I don't have a sleuthing face. You didn't happen to notice what kind of car Melody drives, did you?"

Cornelia shook her head. "Raymond was the car enthusiast. I don't pay cars much attention unless they make a turn without signaling. I hate that. It's so unsafe. And another thing that makes me crazy is . . ."

Jillian let her great-aunt's chatter wash over her as they walked the rest of the way to the car. She realized she ought to be grateful to have the chance to listen to it. *Either one of us could have been hit by the shooter.* That thought made her shudder.

Something deadly was afoot at the theater. Maybe the shooter was aiming at Astoria, but that didn't mean other people couldn't be hurt or even killed, especially with the play's debut fast approaching.

On opening night, nearly everyone Jillian loved was going to be up on the stage and vulnerable, and she had no idea what to do to keep them safe.

Jillian's nerves had her feeling vaguely nauseated from the time she woke up on the day of the first performance. She tried reminding herself that she was only in the play to help keep Cornelia safe, but the thought of stumbling out onto the stage and running into furniture was a real distraction.

At the bakery, it appeared that she was the only person in Moss Hollow who was anticipating the play with dread. Even Bertie admitted to being glad she'd gotten a ticket. "I'm going to sit with Josi," she said as she slipped loaves of fresh bread into bags. "I'd considered getting a ticket near Maudie and Wanda Jean, but those two will probably talk the whole time, and I know Josi knows how to be quiet."

"I wish I was sitting with you," Jillian said bleakly. She twisted ties around the end of each bread bag and put the loaves on a rolling rack to go up front.

Bertie paused and pointed at her. "You're going to be right where you're needed. Since I couldn't talk Cornelia out of being in the play, I feel better knowing someone is backstage with her. I'm going to make sure she doesn't cart those silly tear-out cards along with her. I'll tackle her if I have to."

The image of Bertie tackling her twin sister and wrestling the stack of tear-out cards from her finally broke through Jillian's nerves, and she laughed. "I'd pay money to see that."

"Don't be sassy," Bertie said, though a smile played at the corners of her mouth. "Roll this rack out and fill the bread display, please."

"You got it." Still chuckling a little over the imagined fight, Jillian pushed the rolling rack through the doorway from the kitchen to the customer area.

As Jillian squeezed around the counter to reach the bread display, Maggie asked her if she was nervous about opening night.

"Oh, don't remind me," Jillian said. "My butterflies were napping. I don't need them waking up."

Maggie flapped her hand dismissively and smiled. "You'll do fine."

"I hope we all do great!"

Jillian peeked around the rolling rack to see Bree Weston practically bouncing on her toes. "You must be even more nervous than me, Bree," Jillian said.

"I'm trying to think of it as excited. And I'm drinking lots of tea with honey for my voice." Bree's eyes widened. "Wouldn't that be the worst thing?"

Jillian paused in transferring bagged loaves to the display. "What?"

"If I lost my voice," Bree said.

Jillian thought about Brittany's death, the trapdoor accident, barely avoiding getting run over, and then the bullet that nearly hit Astoria. Bree losing her voice wouldn't be the *worst* thing. Then she realized that her own poor dancing efforts wouldn't be the worst thing either. If they all survived the night, it would be just fine. She smiled encouragingly. "You'll be fine."

"I hope so," Bree said, almost breathlessly. "I heard there will be investors in the audience tonight. I hope they'll be impressed, and we'll be able to keep the theater in town."

"We have to," another customer said. Jillian recognized her as a girl named Hannah, one of the younger dancers from the maids' chorus. "I'm hoping we do lots of plays, and maybe I'll get a big part eventually. I would love to make acting and dancing my career."

With so many people excited about the musical's opening

night, Jillian hoped it would be even a fraction as good as everyone hoped. She whispered a little prayer to that effect as she headed back to the kitchen to tackle the next chore on the order sheet.

Although the day was busy, Bertie shooed Jillian out of the bakery early. "You go home and get some rest before you have to go on tonight. And keep an eye on Cornelia. She's been full of haint talk for days."

Jillian gave her grandmother a hug and agreed. She could practice her dance steps in Belle Haven's nice open foyer, which is exactly what she did.

Cornelia came downstairs while Jillian practiced and offered critique and commentary. Jillian wasn't sure if she found it helpful or distracting. Still, by the time she stopped to go shower and change, she felt a bit better about her upcoming performance.

When it was time to leave, Cornelia suggested Jillian take the wheel again. "That way, I can run my lines while we drive."

"Sounds good."

Bertie, who had arrived home from the bakery about half an hour earlier, caught them before they made it outside. She gave them a stern glare. "You two be careful."

"You're supposed to say 'break a leg,'" Cornelia said.

"No," Bertie said. "I'm not wishing extra trouble on us. Just be careful." Then she gave them each a hug, a rare impulse for Bertie and one that made Cornelia flush with happiness.

When they arrived at the theater, they found the backstage in disarray. Apparently, Porter Logan was missing.

"What am I going to do?" Melody asked, her voice frantic. "I can't have a play without a stage manager."

"When was the last time you saw him?" Jillian asked.

Melody's eyes were wide with panic. "I don't remember. This morning? Maybe last night. Oh, I don't know." She wrung her hands as the actors clustered around her, their faces worried.

"Surely he's here somewhere," Gordon said.

"Maybe he went to get something to eat, and he's a little late," Mrs. Winston added.

The whole group jumped as Astoria's voice cut through the babble. "Shouldn't all of you be doing something constructive in preparation for tonight's show?"

"Porter is missing," Melody said, her voice still full of her near panic.

"I think he may have been frightened away by the ghost," Cornelia said.

Jillian glared at her great-aunt. *Not helpful.*

"I don't think so," Melody said. "Jillian, I asked him about it after you and I talked. He actually believed in the ghost and said he thought Brittany was watching over us. He *liked* the ghost."

"He did?" Jillian suddenly wondered if Porter might have some hand in *being* the ghost. He had seemed angry enough at the funeral to play some cruel jokes. Then she remembered the strange incident when she'd overheard Helene talking to someone who later didn't seem to be there at all. "Melody, are there any hidden passages in this building?"

Melody giggled. "Wouldn't that be fun? But I doubt it. Brittany never mentioned anything like that."

"Enough chatter." Astoria pointed at Melody. "You take over the stage manager duties. Doesn't the director normally just loaf around in the audience on opening night? Tonight you can work instead."

"Well," Melody said fretfully, "I suppose I could if I had Porter's clipboard. It has all the lighting cues and such on it. I could probably muddle through if I had that."

Astoria pointed at Jillian. "Go get it."

Jillian gaped at her. "Me? I have no idea where the clipboard is."

"I'm sure it's in his office," Melody said. "I suppose I could go get it, but I really do have a lot of last-minute things to do. I need to meet with the stagehands, for one."

"Get to it, then," Astoria commanded. "Get everyone ready. This play must run smoothly." Again, she gestured at Jillian. "I told you to go find the silly clipboard. What are you waiting for?"

"Um, directions?" Jillian replied drily. "I have no idea where the man's office is, and the backstage is a maze."

Laura Lee tapped Jillian on the shoulder. "I'll go with you. I know where it is."

Jillian was surprised. "You do?"

Laura Lee rolled her eyes. "In my fortunate position as a sheriff's deputy, I've been part of several backstage searches now."

Astoria clapped her hands. "Less talking, more fetching. You two hurry and get the clipboard." She exhaled theatrically. "Or do I have to do everything?"

No, you stick to bossing people around. Jillian fought the urge to roll her eyes as she followed Laura Lee.

When they reached an empty hallway, Jillian asked Laura Lee if she thought Porter had taken off. "He seemed a strong suspect in the attempted shooting of Astoria. He definitely hates her."

"It's possible," Laura Lee said. "His prints were on the gun, but that doesn't prove anything really. His prints are on everything here since he's the stage manager."

"He struck me as a man angry enough to be violent," Jillian said. "But I can't believe he'd kill Brittany."

"She was taking advantage of his feelings for her," Laura Lee said. "If he worked that out, it would be a pretty strong motive. Apparently, his obsession over Brittany verged on stalking, and stalkers often hear things they don't like."

The hallways were the clearest that Jillian had seen them. Most of the props being used in the play had finally been moved to the wings or onto the stage. The excess had been carried to the storage space under the stage. As a result, only a small bit of overflow cluttered the halls closest to the wings. Jillian and Laura Lee had moved past the clutter well before they got to Porter's office.

The office was small with what appeared to be a thrift-shop metal desk and a worn rolling chair that canted slightly to one side. "They obviously spared no expense in here," Jillian said with a smirk as she crossed to the desk.

Laura Lee stayed in the doorway since two was a crowd in the tiny space. "I noticed that the last time I was in here. I think this might be a converted broom closet."

Jillian picked up a clipboard from the desk and flipped through the pages. It was definitely the one Melody needed. Then she caught sight of the single drawer in the metal desk, which wasn't closed all the way. Jillian spotted something in the visible crack. She walked around the desk and dragged the drawer open. "Look at this."

"What?" Laura Lee asked, stepping into the office.

Jillian held up a small digital recorder. She studied the buttons for a moment, then pressed a button to play back some of the contents. Brittany's irritated voice filled the office, as demanding as ever. "I think we may have found the theater ghost."

"I'd bet you're right." Laura Lee held out her hand, and Jillian dropped the digital recorder into it. "So our stage manager has been playing ghost."

"And the ghost spoke just before the gunshot," Jillian said. "Which certainly makes Porter look good for that."

"And if he's willing to shoot an obnoxious old lady—"

"He might be willing to kill a woman who called him a super creep behind his back."

Laura Lee nodded. "I think we'd better find Porter Logan. It's entirely possible he's not done here."

As they walked back through the halls, Laura Lee called the sheriff's department to pass along what they'd found. Hearing only one side of the conversation was frustrating for Jillian. She desperately wanted reassurances or maybe to hear that the sheriff was shutting down the play. Everyone would be disappointed, but at least they'd be safe.

When Laura Lee finished, she frowned as she shoved the phone back into her pocket. "I'm going out to the parking lot to see if Porter's car is here. You take the clipboard to Melody. As of right now, the play is still on."

"Fine, but I'm sticking to Cornelia like glue."

"I don't think Porter has any reason to hurt her."

"I'll still feel better if I'm watching over her."

They split up, and Jillian hurried to the stage. Melody thanked her repeatedly for the clipboard and clung to it as if it might save her from some awful fate. Jillian took a quick walk through both wings, checking shadowy corners for Porter, then went to the dressing room to watch over Cornelia until the play began.

"Jillian Green, what are you doing in those clothes?" Cornelia scolded the second Jillian walked through the dressing room door. "Why aren't you in costume?"

"I was with Laura Lee, fetching the stage manager's clipboard for Melody," Jillian said. "I guess I can change now."

"I guess you can!" Cornelia huffed, sounding a lot like her sister. "The play will be beginning soon."

Jillian's gaze went to the clock on the wall. She had plenty of time, but she assumed Cornelia's nerves were making her bossy, a thought which brought the return of Jillian's own anxiety.

"Where's Mrs. Winston?" Jillian asked as she pulled the maid's costume from the hanger. "I thought she shared this dressing room with you."

"She is sharing with Bree," Cornelia said with a sniff. "She felt her role was too important to share with me."

Jillian groaned. "This play is making the town crazy."

Cornelia went back to applying heavy makeup. "It is exciting, though. I haven't had this much fun since I was in that movie."

"Don't remind me." Cornelia had nearly been killed when she'd taken part in a movie that was being filmed at Belle Haven, and the memory didn't help Jillian's nerves at all. She took deep breaths and tried to banish the butterflies as she finished changing and worked on her own makeup.

Some of the women in the maids' chorus had minor speaking roles, saying things like, "Yes ma'am," and "For you, sir," but Jillian was happy to have missed out on that. Her own part was little more than scurrying around with a dustcloth and pretending to polish while singing with several other dancers. She ran through the lyrics in her head as she waited in the dressing room with Cornelia.

Later, Jillian couldn't have said if the beginning of the play came too soon or dragged on forever, but she walked to the wings to watch the first scene where Cornelia, as the housekeeper, invited a lost couple—Hunter and Bree—into the home of a wealthy dowager, played by Mrs. Winston.

As she watched over her great-aunt, Jillian had to admit the play was going very smoothly. Other than a few very minor missteps of choreography—probably only noticed by Helene, who was watching the performance from the third row—Jillian couldn't spot any mistakes. And she had never seen Hunter look more handsome or sound more impressive. *I think I could fall in love with him all over again just watching this play.* Her eyes were misty as he sang a particularly sweet song to Bree.

When Jillian's polishing scene came, she ran out onto the stage with Amber and Laura Lee and began dusting furiously. She was glad Amber belted out their song at the top of her lungs, as she was sure it probably drowned out her own squeaky voice. Nerves hadn't helped her singing.

When Cornelia swept on stage to rush them off, Jillian felt the urge to cheer. She only had one more group scene with all the maids in the second act. *I might actually make it through without humiliating myself!*

As the first two acts transpired without issue, Jillian began to feel hopeful for a performance without incident. The disappearance of the stage manager was disconcerting, but Melody seemed to handle his job easily, waving actors on and off the stage with confidence. Finally, the second act ended, and the curtains closed for intermission.

The rest of the actors headed back to their dressing rooms, but Jillian stood in a shadowy corner of the wings debating whether she should go watch Cornelia in the dressing room or keep an eye on the backstage area. If anything dangerous was going to happen, there was only one more act during which it could occur.

While she was pondering, an arm slipped around her waist, making her jump. "Sorry," Hunter said. "I didn't realize you were so lost in thought. Shouldn't you be in your dressing room?"

"I could ask the same of you," Jillian answered. "Shouldn't you be sipping tea with lemon and honey or some other actor thing?"

He chuckled, and Jillian could feel the rumble against her shoulder. "Probably, but being with you calms my nerves. What are you doing back here anyway?"

"Keeping an eye on the wings."

He sighed. "Isn't that more of a job for Laura Lee or one of the deputies?"

"I'm doing my best." This time both Jillian and Hunter jumped, and Laura Lee giggled. "Yeah, you're doing a great job of watching out."

"I was distracted," Jillian said.

Hunter grinned again. "I was the distraction."

"I got that part." Laura Lee cocked a thumb over her shoulder.

"I'm going to the other side of the stage to keep watch. I may be paranoid, but I'm thinking things are going a little *too* well."

"I feel the same way. I'll keep watch on this side." Jillian gave Hunter a little push. "And the lead actor will go back to his dressing room."

"If I must." Hunter bent to give Jillian a peck on the cheek. "Be careful."

Once Hunter and Laura Lee left, Jillian walked around until she spotted Melody sitting on a stool, going over the clipboard of notes. The young woman almost blended in with the shadowy backstage since she'd changed into a black sweater, black jeans, and black boots, an outfit Jillian knew was normal for stage managers who wanted to remain unnoticed.

Melody glanced up as Jillian walked over. "Do you need something?"

"I wanted to tell you that I think you're doing a great job," Jillian said. "The play is going well."

Melody beamed at her. "I think so too. Everyone is working so hard." Then her smile grew even wider and she leaned forward. "I spotted a special surprise guest in the audience. I can barely believe it."

Jillian opened her mouth to ask who it was that Melody had seen, but then she caught sight of movement in the shadows near the edge of the stage. *Is someone messing around over there?* "Excuse me," she said quietly, then hurried over to the shadows where she'd seen the movement. She didn't find anyone, though she did see something glittering on the floor next to the wall. She bent and picked up a delicate silver star. *Where did this come from?*

She suddenly wondered if the silver charm might have come from something of Brittany's. As she remembered, the woman was fond of a lot of jewelry. Jillian turned back to show the charm to Melody, but the stool was empty and the clipboard lay on the floor. Where was she?

Jillian scanned the area. Surely Melody wouldn't have left the clipboard behind. Suddenly Jillian's nerves returned with a chilling fear.

Something was wrong. Very wrong.

Jillian examined the stool carefully, then the floor around it. She spotted some dark scuff marks on the wood. She thought of the heels on Melody's black boots. A person could leave these kinds of marks with those boots. Was Melody trying to leave a trail?

She might have gone off to the bathroom, Jillian reminded herself, admitting that she could be completely overreacting. She truly hoped she was. She followed the scuff marks, hoping to find Melody backstage. The marks were oddly uneven, but if Melody was being dragged, that was only to be expected.

Eventually, the scuff marks led to the stairs going down to the area under the stage. Jillian peered at the darkness below. She wondered if she should get Laura Lee, but she worried that it would be for nothing. There might be a perfectly reasonable answer for Melody's disappearance. Maybe Melody realized they were missing a prop in the stage manager's list, something that had been stored under the stage. Or perhaps Melody was checking the trapdoor elevator. She'd expressed concern about it before, and it would be used in the third act. It was likely she just didn't know she was leaving scuff marks.

Jillian decided to take a peek. If necessary, she could run back upstairs to get help. She descended the steps quietly. At the bottom, she heard voices. She recognized one of them immediately. It was Astoria, sounding as imperious as ever. Clearly, the woman was not under duress. Jillian relaxed slightly. She had been half afraid she would run into Porter Logan in the darkness.

Jillian almost headed back to the wings, but something

made her continue to creep forward instead. *I'll only keep going until I actually see Astoria and Melody. Then I can put my silly imagination completely to rest.*

Between the pieces of furniture scattered around the space and the supports holding up the floor above, Jillian was able to move forward quietly without being spotted, though she would have been hard-pressed to explain exactly why she was being so stealthy.

She peeked around one post and her heartbeat hitched in her chest. Astoria Blaine stood in a small pool of light near the trapdoor elevator. An electric work light had been clipped to the ceiling for the sake of the actor who would be using the elevator in the third act. At the moment, the light illuminated a frightening scene.

Astoria held a gun on a weeping Melody, who stood in the space under the trapdoor. The elevator floor was directly below the trapdoor itself, above Melody's head.

"It was good of your crew to replace our gun for the play," Astoria said. "I had no idea how to get a gun in this backwoods town."

"What are you going to do?" Melody asked.

"It's almost time for your stagehands to test the trapdoor during intermission," Astoria said with a smirk. "It was so helpful of you to insist on a last-minute test. I thought I'd have to drag you down here after the third act began and kill you before a live audience. That would have been a lot riskier with all the actors coming and going." She chuckled. "I guess you did one thing right after all."

"Please don't hurt me," Melody whimpered.

"Hurt you? This is going to be your big death scene. You'll be famous for it. Isn't that what you wanted? To be famous like your dreadful sister?"

"Why?" Melody asked.

"Why the trapdoor?" Astoria asked, intentionally misunderstanding. "I thought it would be poetic, another trapdoor accident like the one I arranged to camouflage Brittany's death.

And to think, it was all inspired by a real accident, the one with that whining teenager."

Melody gawked at Astoria in wide-eyed horror. "You killed your own daughter."

"*Step*daughter," Astoria hissed. "Your sister was draining away my money with all her ridiculous whims. And your father fell for them every single time. I had to put a stop to it, permanently, even if it meant coming down to the back of beyond to do it. Let's just say I realized the world and I would be better off without either of you rotten brats."

A deep male voice spoke from the shadows near Jillian, making her jump. "Those rotten brats are my children."

Astoria spun to stare in shock as a handsome older man stepped out of the shadows and into the pool of light that glinted on his thick, white hair. Laura Lee walked out to stand beside him. The deputy had her own gun drawn. "Put down the gun, Mrs. Blaine."

"Wait," Astoria said, holding up her free hand. "You misunderstand. I was telling Melody that silly story to scare her. I didn't kill Brittany. Porter did it. Everyone knows he hates all of us."

While Astoria babbled, Jillian stepped out from behind the post and motioned for Melody to come to her. Melody quickly scurried out from under the trapdoor elevator and ran to Jillian's side, and Jillian put a protective arm around the trembling woman.

Laura Lee's aim never wavered. "We found Porter. He regained consciousness in the trunk of your car. Did you not know trunks on that model have a release inside? He went straight to the deputy working the parking lot."

"You didn't believe him, did you?" Desperation laced Astoria's words. "He's lying, obviously. He hates our family, I tell you. And he's trying to divert you from his own guilt. He's the one who killed my poor stepdaughter."

"The man's face was covered in blood from the head wound

you gave him," Laura Lee said. "That and the concussion were fairly convincing. You know, he's been a wonderful source of information. He admitted pretending to be a ghost to try to smoke out Brittany's killer. He used some secret doors and passages Brittany had built into the theater. Passages I assume you didn't know about. He admitted to setting the fire in your office to convince you Brittany's ghost was out for vengeance. He was hoping to force you to confess. He even admitted to knocking Gordon on the head to avoid being caught playing ghost in the halls. But he's adamant about one thing. You murdered Brittany."

"No, you have it all wrong," Astoria said. "He killed her, and he was going to kill me and pin Brittany's murder on me. I had to protect myself."

"Fine," Laura Lee said. "Put down your gun, and we'll talk about it."

Astoria was slowly shifting her position. Jillian suspected she was trying to get a better angle to run or maybe get behind the machinery for the elevator. Astoria wasn't pointing her gun at Laura Lee, but she hadn't put it down either.

"You need to drop the weapon *right now*," Laura Lee said.

"Shoot her," Mr. Blaine said coldly. "She killed my daughter. And I believe she may have been trying to poison me as well."

"I didn't kill anyone!" Astoria shrieked. "I'm innocent. It was Porter. It was all Porter."

Jillian realized that Astoria's effort to get behind the heavy machinery that ran the lift had now put her directly below it. How much time had passed? Were the stagehands ready to run their test?

Though Astoria Blaine was clearly a murderer, Jillian desperately did not want to see what would happen if the lift engaged while she stood arguing with Laura Lee. She let go of Melody and darted at Astoria, grabbing the arm that held the gun and dragging her out from under the trapdoor lift.

At that very instant, the mechanism ground to life, and the elevator rolled down into the place Astoria had stood only moments before. Unfortunately, the moving platform also obscured Laura Lee's aim, and Astoria struggled to pull her arm free while Jillian held on tight, keeping the gun pointed at the floor.

"Jillian!" Laura Lee yelled. "Get out of the way."

Good idea, Jillian thought, but there was no way she was letting go of the woman's gun hand now that she was so close to her.

"I should have run you over when I had the chance!" Astoria snarled as she fought Jillian.

Then the gun went off, and Astoria screamed shrilly as the bullet went right through the pointed tip of her expensive high heel. She dropped the gun and would have fallen if Jillian hadn't had a tight grip on her arm.

"I'm shot!" Astoria yelled.

Laura Lee kicked the gun out of the way as she closed the distance to Jillian and Astoria. "You'll live," she said. "Which is more than I can say for your daughter."

"*Step*daughter," Astoria snarled through gritted teeth.

Before Laura Lee led Astoria away, she told Jillian that she'd run into Mr. Blaine in the wings after she'd gotten word about Porter, and he'd insisted on going along on the search for his remaining daughter. They soon discovered the fallen clipboard and followed the same clues as Jillian.

Jillian watched the old man walking up the steps holding

Melody's hand. Even with her makeup a teary mess, Melody was glowing.

With Astoria in custody, the play went on after an extended intermission. Laura Lee had to miss the maids' last big dance number, but Jillian still danced in it, though her costume was a bit worse for wear after her tussle with Astoria. She nearly ran into Amber French once, but she made it through with limited embarrassment overall.

After her dance number, Jillian stood in the wings near Melody. She snuck a glance at the young woman beside her. Though she still seemed a bit pale and shaken, Melody had followed Porter's notes without a hitch. Jillian was quite impressed with her—and very glad she hadn't turned out to be a murderer.

"You're doing great," she whispered to Melody.

Melody pointed toward the stage with the clipboard. "It's all them." Then she beamed at Jillian. "My father said he's going to keep the theater. This play is just the first of many."

Though Jillian was pretty sure that her acting career was over, she was happy for the younger woman, who deserved to be passionate about something after everything she'd gone through.

Jillian shifted her attention to watch the rather overdramatic revealing of the play's murderer. Gordon hammed it up shamelessly as he recited his monologue boasting of his villainy, even going so far as to twirl his mustache. Jillian grinned. Gordon seemed to be taking his latest ladylove's arrest well.

Then Hunter gave the last lines of the play, an impassioned declaration of love. Melody gestured toward a stagehand to close the curtain. The audience broke into thunderous applause as the curtain swept shut.

Jillian straightened the seams of her costume and prepared to run out with the rest of the maids for their curtain call. She felt a swell of pride at the amazing job everyone had done.

On cue, she trotted onto the stage and looked out at the audience with a smile so wide that it strained the edges of her mouth. They'd done it. They'd gotten through the play, and everyone she loved was safe.

After the last curtain call, when the whole cast held hands and bowed together, Jillian stood behind the closed curtain with her palm on her chest. She was slightly out of breath from the excitement of it all. As she willed her nerves to calm down, she felt a warm hand on her arm.

She smiled up at Hunter as the rest of the cast hurried off to the wings. "You were wonderful," she told him. "You're lucky I'm not the jealous type, because you were doing an awfully good job of playing a man in love."

"That's because it wasn't acting," he said. "I am a man in love. All I had to do was think of you."

Heat flooded Jillian's cheeks. "I love you too."

"In that case . . ." To her utter amazement, Hunter dropped to one knee right on the scuffed stage and reached into the pocket of his costume's jacket. "Singing about love all this time has made me realize I don't want to go one more day without asking you to be mine forever. You're my perfect fit. I love you more with every passing day, and I want to spend the rest of my life with you." He held up a ring, his eyes shining with hope and adoration. "Jillian Green, will you marry me?"

Jillian put her hand to her mouth and blinked back the tears that prickled her eyes. She'd had no idea he was planning to ask her to marry him, and frankly, would never have admitted to anyone that she'd known what her answer would be all along. But now, in this moment, she didn't hesitate in her response. "Yes!"

Hunter slipped the ring on her finger, and applause burst from both wings. Jillian smiled down at the gorgeous emerald-cut diamond set in platinum, which sparkled even in the dim light.

I'm getting married!

Hunter rose to his feet and took her hand. "I hope you like it," he murmured. "Bertie helped me pick it out weeks ago."

"I love it," Jillian said breathlessly. "But not nearly as much as I love you."

"I had all these plans for a grand proposal, but—"

"Oh hush." Jillian put her hand on his cheek. "I wouldn't change a thing."

Suddenly the curtains swept open, but Hunter didn't seem to care. He wrapped Jillian in an ardent embrace and kissed her thoroughly, inspiring another burst of applause. This time, it sounded like all of Moss Hollow joined in.

They've been waiting a long time for this, Jillian thought with amusement as she returned Hunter's kiss. *And, honestly, so have I.*

Shoofly Die
Book Twenty Two Recipe

Savannah's Shoofly Pie

Ingredients

¾ cup water
⅔ cup molasses
1 teaspoon baking soda
1 egg, beaten
1½ cups flour

¾ cup dark brown sugar
½ cup cold butter, cubed
½ teaspoon cinnamon
9-inch unbaked piecrust

Directions

1. Preheat oven to 400 degrees.

2. In a saucepan, bring water to boiling. Stir in molasses. Return to a boil, then remove from heat. Let cool until barely warm, then stir in baking soda and beaten egg. Keep stirring until smooth.

3. Combine flour and brown sugar in a medium bowl. Cut in butter to make coarse crumb mixture.

4. Pour one third of the molasses mixture into the unbaked crust. Add one third of the crumb mixture. Continue adding in layers, ending with the crumb mixture on top.

5. Bake for 10 minutes. Reduce heat to 350 degrees and bake for 35 minutes. Allow to cool before cutting. Serve with whipped cream or vanilla ice cream.

Up to this point, we've been doing all the writing. Now it's *your* turn!

Tell us what you think about this book, the characters, the bad guy, or anything else you'd like to share with us about this series. We can't wait to hear from *you*!

Log on to give us your feedback at:
https://www.surveymonkey.com/r/ChocolateShoppe

Annie's FICTION

Learn more about Annie's fiction books at

AnniesFiction.com

We've designed the Annie's Fiction website especially for you!

Access your e-books and audiobooks • Manage your account

Choose from one of these great series:

Amish Inn Mysteries	Chocolate Shoppe Mysteries
Annie's Attic Mysteries	Creative Woman Mysteries
Annie's Mysteries Unraveled	Hearts of Amish Country
Annie's Quilted Mysteries	Inn at Magnolia Harbor
Annie's Secrets of the Quilt	Secrets of the Castleton Manor Library
Annie's Sweet Intrigue	Scottish Bakehouse Mysteries
Antique Shop Mysteries	Victorian Mansion Flower Shop Mysteries

What are you waiting for? Visit us now at **AnniesFiction.com!**